Fall like Lightning

Fall like Lightning

D. Benedict Thyagarajan

LITHOUSE
2020

Fall like Lightning— — published by Lithouse, Delhi.

© Author, 2020

ISBN: 978-93-88945-40-0

Laser typeset by
Lithouse, Delhi.

Dedication

This book is dedicated to the person who taught us to kneel and pray for everything.

This book is the last ambitious and zealous work of the author. He was so determined and eager in completing this book that he spent many sleepless and anxious nights overlooking most of his health concerns to the point that he even ignored serious conditions such as bleeding ears and loss of sense in certain parts of his body. This was not revealed even to the family, except to the all-knowing and ever faithful Lord in prayer who always remained his companion in his pain and tribulations.

His life was an apt expression of love towards his greatest love-The Lord, whom he dedicated his entire life, placing all his troubles at his feet day and night.

The Lord too never left him alone, as he carried his Cross each day with complete faith to obtain the greatest love, he desired and received all his life from the Lord.

The Lord was always faithful to our dearest father as he gave him enough endurance to finish this last piece of work and as he laid his pen to rest, the Lord very lovingly allowed his servant to lay and rest in eternal glory on 14 January 2019.

Great is Thy love Oh Lord

and great are Thy children

Whom you have chosen for

Thy greatest works!!

Daughters

Contents

Foreword

Screenplay written on the life and mighty works of Prophet Elijah, in obedience to the will of God, as the Holy Bible. This has been written, hoping some one from some corner of the world will be inspired to shoot this as a movie, for the greater glory of God, and for his Kingdom of justice, peace and joy on the Earth, which is the only hope for humanity, assured in the Holy Bible.

Amy

Preface

I happened to read an elaborate article from an old copy of 'The Illustrated Weekly of India' by a former Union Minister, a great intellect, author and a well-known journalist(Name not disclosed). I was greatly surprised to see that the article was based on Christian theology. He had painstakingly gone through the Bible and many commentaries to publish this remarkable article. While going through it, I found this article was very critical about certain biblical facts. To be very specific, he was unable to relish some of the events in the life of Prophet Elijah. The writer considered Elijah as a religious fanatic, who ordered the slaughtering of almost 450 prophets of Baal. He considered this as genocide and Elijah a mass murderer, due to religious fanaticism.

It is not only this writer, but for many Bible reading Christians the slaughter of the prophets of Baal and burning of the two contingents of soldiers, fifty in each under a Captain, by the order of Elijah may be difficult to accept. Therefore, there is nothing unusual in the understanding of Elijah, negatively. This cloud remained in my own mind for several years. However, I learnt to prayerfully think and meditate on the difficult areas in the Bible, which find no explanation from the Bible Commentaries.

What made the writer critical and negative on Prophet Elijah? Later, I understood his reasoning and realized Elijah stands as the tallest and greatest of all the prophets of God.

This Screenplay *'Fall like lightning'* has been written to present a clear picture about the great Prophet Elijah and to highlight how God used Elijah for his redemption plan, for the entire human race.

Being born in India, a country with 86% of the population as Hindus, Indian students, irrespective of their religion ,were made to study the biographies of Hindu saints and their poetical works- the well-known devotional hymns, written in highly scholarly language, in the curriculum of studies, at least up to class X. In fact, these were prescribed for character building, as well as, introducing spiritual life to the students. This made me seriously study other major religions, especially Hinduism and Islam. I have my personal library full of such works; to mention some of them, I have commentaries of Dr. S. Radhakrishnan and Sadhu TL Vaswani on Bhagwat Gita. Also, I have six versions of the Holy Quran (one in Tamil, which I consider as the best of all the six versions of the Holy Quran, in English.) With this background my observations and comments may not be totally incorrect. I cannot write or analyse all religions. Therefore, I would like to confine to Hinduism, which is familiar to most Indians.

Some of the Hindu saints were kings and wealthy business men, even generals in the army of these kings, who ruled different Provinces. In those days, Religion, Philosophy and Humanity were mixed in their devotional hymns, written in poetical language. Poetical hymns were considered as the best form of expression of spiritual experiences during those days.

Some of these major themes of these devotional hymns were, renunciation of world's power and glory and accepting the life of wandering sages, singing the glory of god. Their hymns educated the people on humility, to consider one's self as lower than all human beings, and not to claim any superiority over any single human beings on earth, on any pretext. One more dominant theme was on peaceful co-existence and not harming any human beings, but always serve fellow human beings as humble servants. Greed for wealth, robbing others properties, murdering weak fellow human beings, were all considered as unpardonable sins, in those devotional hymns. There is a well-known poetical verse by a Hindu saint in Tamil *Ondre Kulam, Oruvane Devan*, which means "Only one human race and one God". Also there were several Hindu saints to guide the people, not to attach themselves to the perishable or the visibly seen glories of the world but to detach themselves and attach only to the God Almighty. However, Satan the devil entered and brought many divisions, and ultimately brought violence and sexual crimes, when people loved and cared for each other and when there was total absence of sex crimes of any sort; nor fights and murders for wealth!? Therefore, the ancient guiding dictum of Hinduism was *Satyameve Jayate*; which means 'Truth Triumphs'. Now, all these beautiful ways of life and the noble principles are lessened or in low ebb, due to changes brought by the evil forces headed by the devil. It is not only Hinduism, but other major religions have undergone such assaults by the evil one, therefore, some negative changes have become realities. As the form of expression of devotion was in poetical form among the Hindus, there was a galaxy of Hindu saints who contributed to the spiritual treasure of Hinduism, in classical, poetical tones. I would like to quote few verses of one of my beloved Hindu Saint Thayumanavar. He has put two essentials of Hindu philosophy in two verses. *Avanarulal Avanai Pottri* "Praising and worshipping him by his grace" He means without God's grace no one can worship him. No self-effort, but grace from God alone can enable one to worship God. In another couplet he writes, *Anbar Pani seyya... ennai aalakki vittuvittal Inba nilai thanaga vandhidume Parabarame.* If you change my whole personality, to serve others, humbly, I am sure to attain the supreme bliss of heaven." The essence of these few verses mean, humility is the foundation of Hindu spiritual life. Total surrender to God and total service to every human being created by God.

Satan did not even spare Science and Technology, two adverse major contributions are, incurable skin diseases with the advent of pornography and the availability of porno items through cell phones, which resulted in debauchery, divorces, rapes murders etc.; and turned people into liars. It was not so, when landline telephone services were the only communication facility. The same Science and Technology has been many times mindlessly used by scientists. Real Estate agents are the major contributors of artificial earthquakes on the surface level by digging and drilling the earth for their construction. Human life is no safer, in the present age; and people are more worried about their survival and less about their precious souls.

To add to our horrors and terrors; thousands of people have met their sudden deaths due to accidents; and collusion of ships and sub-marines in the oceans; due to technical snags because of, nuts, bolts, screws, tires, petrol etc. All such unimaginable disasters have certainly caused death blows to spirituality since life has become uncertain and very cheap. Only God can save the whole human race from the abuse of Science and Technology.

Coming to Christian faith, the ways and means, Satan the devil has been using from the period of Genesis and at the time of Elijah; and now more rigorously in the modern age are great warnings or wake up calls for the faithful or God's people, to escape from the traps of Satan.

Coming back to Prophet Elijah to clear some of the critical views of the writer of The illustrated weekly, I am using fictitious events and dialogues among the teachers (Rabbis) from the School of Prophets at Gilgal, Bethel and Jericho in this Screenplay, to explain the set up and the situation to bring out the truth. Also, I allow the crowds to speak, here and there, for the same purpose. These are fictitious dialogues and set ups, with no such reference in the Holy Bible. My only purpose for such application is, to make people understand, clearly, the underlying facts or behind the scenes factors of those references in the Holy Bible. The Bible scholars and the theologians would prefer to use the dialogue between God and the prophets or the people, as per the Holy Bible 'undiluted' to write anything. But it would not be enough to expose the prevailed situations of that period since so many events are narrated bluntly, leaving the readers to understand or imagine. This may differ from individual to individual. The normal practice is accepting the blunt statements, as it is in the form, without understanding the cause and situation but the major problem is, most of the people cannot understand anything about the past and present in respect of such cryptic statements. It does not mean, I am trying to make   additions in the Holy Bible, which cannot be accepted by any Bible scholars or believers, rather would come under the clause of blasphemy. But one fact needs special emphasis here, the Holy Bible in our hands is, nothing but based on 'Oral Tradition' or orally transmitted facts and events, from one generation to another till the age of any form of writings came into existence; and more importantly in printing Technology. Therefore, I am using the crowds of the Bible and the Rabbis of the three Schools of Prophets to speak on the events of those years through the fictitious dialogue, in order to understand the events and situations, clearly. However, I have given uttermost importance to such dialogues as per the Holy Bible, between God and his servants, which are reproduced, as it is in form, without adding even an iota to such dialogue. Also, I have re-produced few small scenes, as it is in the Holy Bible, which can be easily identified.

As a screenplay, I felt the need to add some scenes and dialogues through the negative characters such as Jezebel and the Baal worshippers, who alone can qualify any screenplay to be shot as a movie, that too, in the present world. (I added a pinch of modern corruptions for a cocktail!) Moreover, I have not penned this Screenplay, exclusively, for the pious people; rather to catch the attention of the people leading loose lives! But the pious and holy people remain as they were, even in this Screenplay, untouched.

Idol worship and devil worship referred in the time of Elijah was basically unspiritual way of worship inspired by the evil spirit, demanding earthly things like wealth and properties and also for gratification of sexual desires of loose life and also demanding curses on their enemies due to jealousy, human sacrifice, liquor, gold and silver to please their idols or devils to practice witchcraft, sorcery and black magic etc. which should not be mixed with the worship of idols in the Hindu temples. These are no more known as Idols but 'Murtis' or deities. The Hindus worship them as living deities with whom they can communicate and receive spiritual blessings; and not demanding the earthly glories with greed for money and wealth. Nor practicing witchcraft or black magic in their community. Hindus worship most devoutly idols, statues of their deities in the temples of Madurai, Tirupati, Kanchipuram, Chidambaram and all over India. It is their spiritual way of worship, with unparalleled devotion and dedication. They take high risk 'Kailash Yatra' to reach Kedarnath of Uttarakhand and Mansarovar and Gangotri. They undergo instant spiritual bliss while worshipping in these temples for, several thousand years. Hinduism has its own philosophy in this regard. "Vasudeva Kudumbagam" "All must live happily" are the prayers of Hindus following ancient Hinduism.

Also, in modern times, the usage of words like heathenism and paganism are no more in vogue, due to the plurality of social structure.

The philosophy is, if everyone practices one's own religion, seriously and sincerely, the present world wild become a heaven with peace, joy and love; totally disallowing violence and corruption of any sort.

IMPORTANT NOTE -

This Screenplay has been written based on the life and ministry of Elijah at a period of the biblical History, as per the prevailing Religious and socio-political circumstances. Therefore, this Screenplay is nowhere connected to any of the contemporary religious or socio-political circumstances. There is neither any criticism or approval or disapproval on the present-day circumstances. This Screenplay has been written to have an overview on the past, to grasp anything good for the whole humanity- specifically for World Peace!

- Author

Scene 1

Prophet Elijah –
A Man of Sorrow
School of Prophets at *Bethel*

Rabbis and students of the schools of Bethel, Gilgal and Jericho visit each other's school, despite the long distances, in turn, once in a year to share their experiences the health of the spiritual and moral life of the Chosen People, who were spread, here and there.

During such visits they may be updating the events taking place, concerned with the Chosen People, God's people; and focusing more on the prophets and their efforts to guide them as per the divine law; and also to warn them as when they receive any message from the Lord to correct themselves, to ensure that the People of God live their lives, as per the Commandments of God. I am making these fictitious scenes and dialogues to bring out the History, to feel it alive. We must take it for granted that such travels of the servants of God had taken place, to share information with each other. Moreover, almost all servants of God from Abraham to Moses and all the prophets and servants of God were travelers searching for new pastures and lands. Even for that matter Jesus Christ, himself, was also a great traveler in spreading the Kingdom of God.

I have written few chapters on the Sharing Sessions of the senior Rabbis from the School of Prophets from Bethel, Gilgal and Jericho with their students and active citizens. Some of these chapters have few lengthy dialogues and repeated references. I found no other way to narrate the events and their implications on the people and their spiritual life, which are historical.

I did not add any glamour or intellectual and artificial scent to this Screen Play, to capture special attention or to complete with professional screen play writers. I have kept in mind that I am writing this screen play, which is Bible based.

The Chief Rabbi of Bethel invites the Chief Rabbi from Jericho to preside over the Session.

Chief Rabbi of Bethel: May all honour and glory be to our Lord. I greet every one of you in the Holy name of Jehovah. May God bless every one of you, who took the pain to travel long distances to take part in this time of sharing to update us on the matters pertaining to the people of God. I invite the Chief Rabbi of Jericho to come and preside over this session and deliver the keynote address which will be followed with discussions and sharing. Thank you (Bowing down he invites the Chief Rabbi of Jericho; they hug each other and greet with love).

Chief Rabbi of Jericho: I thank the Chief Rabbi of Bethel for giving me this honour to preside over this session. May the Lord guide us during our sharing and discussions(smiling).

If anyone of you desire to say something during my speech you can do so by raising your hand (on my way I met Prophet

Elijah). He looked like a man of sorrow carrying a heavy burden of the people of God, who have turned away from Jehovah, the true God of Israel and following Baal and following all those demoralizing rituals offered to Ashtoreth. Hearing about the apostasy and all those sacrileges and blasphemies resulted in idol worship all happened because of the present ruler of Israel, King Ahab.

His father Omri, the founder of Samaria brought evil in the eyes of the Lord. He did more to provoke the Lord God of Israel to anger than all the kings of Israel that were before them. He boldly led the people into heathenism by setting aside the worship of Jehovah and switching over to Baal worship. This high pitch is mainly due to his unlawful action. I mean marrying outside our community with the daughter of Ethbaal, King of Ziodinians, the high priest of Baal. This marriage with an idolatrous woman abhorred by the Lord and resulted disastrously both to himself and to the nation. Israel wandered far from the living God and corrupted their ways before him. The dark shadow of apostasy covered the whole land with images of Baalism and Ashtoreth everywhere.

Chief Rabbi of Gilgal: (raises his hand and speaks). Here I would like to add some information. Ahab is weak morally. So, using his weak character his wife Jezebel despicable Sidonian princess introduced and propagated the religion and culture of Canaanite gods in Israel chiefly of Baal and Ashtoreth. She could easily mould Ahab's character to do everything possible to wipe out Yahweh worship in Israel. King Ahab began to worship Baal and build a temple for Baal in Samaria and set up an altar for Baal. He made an Asherah pole. King Ahab did everything that could make the Lord angry even more than any of the kings of Israel who ruled before him. Not only did his wife Jezebel convert King Ahab but she went ahead for mass conversion of the Israelites by tempting them with immoral acts of sexual orgies, temple prostitution, degrading pleasures of sensual pleasures as worship. So, with these traps the Israelites rejected the worship of their true God Jehovah and became worshippers of Baal and Ashtoreth. Whatever was abhorred by the God of Israel as sin and forbidden were adopted by the Israelites. I heard that the wicked woman, Jezebel herself as a seductress, vivacious promotes sexual orgies which is accepted by those women and considered a favourite ritual of Ashtoreth, Goddess of Fertility. Also there are unbelievable stories of homosexuality and lesbianism as special offerings to Baal and Ashtoreth. Most horrible news are they do not spare even young girls below the age of ten by these beasts, as special acts to please their gods. As per the heathen's belief the Baals are fertility gods, masters of life, sex, rain and harvest. The worship of Baal is coupled with cultic prostitution.

Most of the Israelites were lured into this pagan culture. Those who have gone astray prostituted their bodies in sex openly showing their infidelity to Yahweh. Another practice of these pagan cults was human sacrifice. Heil of Bethel sacrificed his son Abirma his first born to rebuild Jericho. And at the time of laying the foundation for the cursed city and when he set up the gates of the city, he sacrificed his youngest son, Segub to please Baal.

All these immoral acts are spreading like wild fire into the whole nation and Israel has gone far away from the redeeming hand of Yahweh.

Chief Rabbi of Bethel: (raises his hand to speak). I too have something to add. Ever since Ahab has become the ruler there is unrest and fear psychosis gripping the whole nation founded by God to preserve the pure race in order to guide the future human race towards moral and spiritual way of life. Idol worshippers are patronized by the ruler Ahab and his wife Jezebel. They are immensely happy, but the worst sufferers are the remnant people who still worship only one God, Yahweh revealed to the great servant of God, Moses and our patriarchs, Abraham, Isaac, Jacob. The remnant is left with no other choice but to worship Yahweh in secret, but they are being persecuted and suppressed everywhere in Israel. (Visuals of persecution to be shown).

They are being forced to accept Baal and Ashtoreth as the gods created the sun and moon and controlling the bounties of heaven, running brooks, the streams of living water the gentle dew, hills and valleys, streams and fountains, the sun and the clouds of heaven and all the powers of nature. All these have been created and controlled by Baal and Ashtoreth. This is the new faith generated by Queen Jezebel with the approval of her husband King Ahab. So to say there is total moral collapse and all the efforts of Yahweh in guiding the Israelites from Egypt to the present land have been spoiled by Ahab and his wife Jeze bel.

Rabbi of Jericho (raises his hand to speak). I would like to sum up whatever has been narrated by me and the other two Chief Rabbis of Bethel and Gilgal. These are the burdens more severely felt by the man of God, Elijah who is pondering day and night and anxiously waiting for the intervention of Yahweh to put an end to the rule of devil worshippers. One measure of his stature is to be found in the fact that he was the man raised by God at the time that Baal worship threatened the very existence of the worship of Yahweh in Israel turning it an idolatrous nation to bring the wrath of God who has power to create and also to destroy. The Chosen people have already started breaking the Ten Commandments received through Moses. They no more honour God nor love him with their heart, soul, body and mind. They deny Jehovah as true God. Sabbath has been no more in their memory. They throw away their parents to the streets, murder for anything and everything has become law of life. They do much more than adultery, stealing and giving false witness has become source for living. No one is without guilt of eyeing a neighbor's wife, or neighbor's wealth. The opposite what God of Israel that the people be faithful to their Creator and also faithful to their neighbors in following the Commandments but now they have their new commandments from their god Baal and sex goddess Ashtoreth to lead demoralized lives like animals.

These changes are taking place under King Ahab and Queen Jezebel overburdening the sorrows of prophet Elijah on the people of God. Jezebel the seductress queen schemed diabolically to make all Israelites break the Law given through Moses more importantly all the Ten Commandments. The Israelites now in the grip of Jezebel are polluted and beyond recovery with their worship of Baal and Ashtoreth and offering filthy rituals corrupting their own souls. Yahweh the true and only God from the beginning warned the Israelites through his prophets.

"Come out from among them. Be ye separate to walk as children of light never to be yoked with the unbelievers because there could be no fellowship with righteousness and unrighteousness and there can be no communion with light and darkness." Therefore, there are reasons for the prophet of God, Elijah to be more burdened in his soul by seeing God's people going astray. Let us also share the burden of prophet Elijah and pray that God will guide him in his prophetic ministry, Amen.

Scene 2

The Dramatic Declaration of Elijah

Details of the scene: King's Royal Court at Samaria

Clad in coarse garments, usually, worn by the prophets of that time Elijah travelled day and night until he reached Samaria to deliver heaven's message to Ahab, entrusted by the Lord.

Elijah arrives at the palace, and passes through the guards and the officials. He appears before King Ahab, who is in the Royal court, surrounded by high officials and generals, more than them, his wife Jezebel beside him in the throne.

Elijah does not greet the King but goes straight into action. **Elijah:** (Lifting up his hand towards heaven and delivers the message). As the Lord God of Israel lives whom I serve, there will be neither dew nor rain in the next few years except at my word.

(The King and the Queen and everyone present were aghast for few seconds. That time was good enough for the prophet to disappear from that Royal Court, swiftly as he entered in same manner, leaving them shocked).

King Ahab: (Angry and losing his temper gets up from his royal seat). Who is that rogue? Hurry up and find out and get him here or find out his details. How dare he utter such words of curses upon the nation before me? He didn't bow down before me to accept my royal position as king of Israel nor did he introduce himself. (He looks at the guards at the entrance furiously). Why didn't you check him or catch him and bring him to me? Were you sleeping? (Turning to the Captain in charge of guards). Captain, suspend these guards from service.

Queen Jezebel: Cursed be that man who uttered curses to block the treasures of heaven. He must not be left to live, he must be caught and brought for trial to impose a death sentence on him. (Calls the prophets of Baal in the Royal Court). you also jointly curse that man with punishments from Baal to our god of rain and all treasures of heaven.

Prophets of Baal (cursing in chorus): Yes, let him be doomed and struck by lightning and killed. We also curse that man who delivered such message which was not from our god Baal. Let our god Baal bring disasters upon the man who delivered such a message to our King and Queen and to the entire nation.

(Turmoil erupts in the Royal Court. A Captain with hundred soldiers mount on their horses and rush in all directions to catch hold of the offender).

Sub Scene 'Word of God to Elijah'

The moment Elijah left the Royal Court -the Word of God comes to Elijah.

Voice from Heaven (ordering him) Leave here, turn eastward and hide in the Kerith Ravine, east of the Jordan. You will drink from the brook, and I have ordered the ravens to feed you there.

(Elijah obeys the Divine command of God and his presence, with utmost reverence and love then unlocking from that supernatural experience he gets into action, to reach the destination, where God had ordered him to go).

Sub Scene: Travel Scene

On his way to Samaria, Elijah passes through the overflowing streams, hills and valleys covered with verdure, and stately forests that seem beyond the reach of drought.

Elijah continues his journey to reach Kerith Ravine, east of the Jordan. He finds the brook Cherith. Elijah settles down at the brook and drinks fresh water. He is lonely. Suddenly, ravens miraculously bring bread and meat. Elijah eats them thanking God and the ravens. The ravens continue bringing him bread and meat in the morning and in the evening. The ravens feed Elijah, as per the word of God. He looks at them thankfully. They fly off after leaving him with bread and meat.

Sub Scene

Again, to the Royal Court of Ahab

Like a thunderbolt from the sky, the message of impending judgment fell upon the ears of the wicked king. Before he could recover from the shock, Elijah had disappeared from the scene. Jezebel takes on the role of Ahab to deal tough with the offender.

Jezebel: I order in the name of the king that all the prophets of Baal and Ashtoreth should immediately assemble before Baal's Temple (The message reaches rapidly, and all the prophets reach the Temple).

Jezebel: (The Queen addresses the congregation of prophets, right in front of the weak and morally bankrupt King Ahab).

We have to consider whatever is spoken by the Prophet of Jehovah as utter foolishness. His curse for a drought on the whole country is an act of sedition. Therefore, he must be arrested and brought as early as possible for a trial and also to make him understand before his death that Baal is the god responsible for rain and dew and all fertility of our country. We have a female goddess in Ashtoreth whom we worship for fertility, sexual prowess and war. So, we have such great powers protecting and providing us. Therefore, I order all the priests to arrange immediate rituals to please our god and goddess to nullify the curse of that unknown entity in the name of an unknown entity god. This is an opportunity to prove Baal and goddess Ashtoreth as true gods and not Jehovah and to prove the word of Elijah as false. Baal could still give dew and rain causing the streams to continue to flow and vegetation to flourish. Then let the King of Israel understand this truth and worship Baal more faithfully and let him set an example for the people of Israel to follow him to worship Baal as their god and not the God of Elijah.

Prophets of Baal and Ashtoreth in chorus: Yes your majesty our Queen, we will obey you and immediately begin to perform rituals to please our god and goddess, Baal and Ashtoreth. We will do everything to turn the curse of that mad man to a great blessing from Baal and Ashtoreth with plenty of rain and dew.

Scene 3

Agonizing Prophets of Baal

One year passes without rain and the streams drying up and the signs of famine are seen in the whole country of Israel.

The weeping prophets in one chorus: Oh, our god, Baal and goddess Ashtoreth you were so generous by sending plenty of rain during the seasons in the past. What made you angry not to send rain during the past one year? We are suffering without water there is no water in the streams, our farm lands have turned waste lands. Oh, Baal please rescue and send rain immediately oh Ashtoreth, please recommend our case with Baal to get rain.

Worshippers of Baal: (in one chorus). Oh! our God, Baal please hear our prayers and appeals of our prophets and send rain before we die, have mercy on us. Please do not delay any more.

One prophet of Baal: Lord Baal are you angry and stopped rain just because some of your worshippers had gone astray and joined Jehovah worshippers? We are ready to send our brutal force to bring back those misguided people and we will re-convert them to worship you. And if they insist to go back to join Jehovah worshippers. We will kill them in front of you. Are you satisfied now? Lord Baal, please send rain.

Chief prophet of Baal: Yes, yes this could be one of the reasons for Lord Baal to be angry with great difficulty we convinced the Jehovah worshippers to become Lord Baal worshippers. It looks now they believe in the word of Elijah the prophet of Jehovah and so they deserted Lord Baal, but we will not leave them if they do not come back to become Lord Baal worshippers, we will kill them with their whole families.

Then the rituals begin to please Baal and Ashtoreth. Young naked women come and dance before Baal. And young naked men come and dance before goddess Ashtoreth, the goddess of sex and fertility. Then some of the prophets bring barrels of liquor and pour on the idols of Baal and Ashtoreth. The people bend down and lick the liquor flowing down from the idols and get drunk. Some prophets bring animals and slaughter before the idols and the un-skinned flesh of the animals are roasted and served for the drunken worshippers. After eating the roasted flesh the young men and women get into sex acts to please Baal and Ashtoreth.

Woman worshipper: Oh dear God Baal we all know that the best way of pleasing you and to obtaining your blessings is sex in front of you because you like it too keeping sex and fertility goddess Ashtoreth closer to you Sure you both may indulge in sex after we leave you in privacy.

Man worshipper: Yes, yes also you are more interested to watch gang sex few men on one woman. Hey guys come on let us grab this woman and enjoy gang sex before our God. Baal it may please him to send rain to us. (So, four to five men fall on that one woman to have sex one after one with her. She responds very happily for such gang sex).

A man after sex with that woman: I have finished I am sure God Baal is very happy for my sexual prowess. Now you get into sex with this woman to make Baal and Ashtoreth happier. Happy (He calls another man from that group to have sex).

(Those men finish their animal acts with that woman).

One person suddenly jumps and screams like evil spirit possessed maniac and announces loudly, "I am going to offer my son to Baal I am going to cut my son into pieces in front of Baal and pour his blood on him as special ritual."

(So, he does whatever he said and offers the human sacrifice that too by cutting his ten-year-old son in front of Baal, places his dead body before Baal and collects the blood from his son's body and pours it on the head of Baal).

(Visuals of Human Sacrifice).
With all these, beastly way of heathen worship and human sacrifice, nothing falls from the sky except the scorching heat and total famine people are suffering miserably and finding no relief of any sort.

Scene 4

Ravens Feed Elijah

Elijah spends few months at the brook of Kerith Ravine. All these months, he was miraculously provided with food by the ravens. The ravens brought meat for Elijah. They became friendly with Elijah. They had flown down from unknown destinations, came and sat on his shoulder with meat. Elijah received them thankfully and ate. However, due to the continued drought and famine across the country, the brook became dry. When Elijah was in a confused condition the Word of God comes to him.

The Voice of God: Arise go at once to Zarephath of Sidon and stay there. I have commanded a widow in that place to supply you with food.

Sub Scene: Elijah meets the Widow of Zarephath

Elijah bows down and touches the ground with his fore head, as submission to God's command. Then, he walks down towards Zarephath, a heathen land. When he was approaching the town gate, he finds a widow gathering sticks. Elijah calls her respectfully as per their custom and asks her.

Elijah: The would you bring me a little water in a jar, so I may have a drink? (With her bodily language she accepts his request and moves to bring him water. Elijah interrupts). Also I pray thee bring me, please, a piece of bread."

(The woman is not an Israelite but a believer in the true God and lived a life of a believer all her life, like any other Israelite woman).

The widow (In very pathetic voice). I don't have any bread only a handful of flour in a jar and a little oil in a jug. I am gathering a few sticks to take home and will make a meal for myself and my son (with tears rolling down from her eyes). that we may eat and die.

(No greater test of faith than this could have been required). The widow had hitherto treated all strangers with kindness. Now regardless of the suffering that might result on herself and her child and trusting in the God of Israel to supply her every need, she met this supreme test of hospitality according to the saying of Elijah. Wonderful was the hospitality shown to God's prophet by this Phoenician woman, and wonderfully her faith and generosity rewarded.

Elijah (With confident voice). Don't be afraid, go home and do as you have said. But first make a small cake and bread for me from what you have and bring it to me then make something for your son and yourself. For this is what the Lord the God of Israel says, The jar of flour will not be used up and the jug of oil will not run dry until the day the Lord gives rain on the land.

The widow: Let it be so by the grace of your God. Please wait I will go and cook cake and bread for you. You may be hungry due to travel. The widow prepares cake and bread and serves.

Widow: Please have your bread and cake. (Elijah goes for atraditional hand wash before having the meal and returns to eat the meal).

(Visuals of widow feeding prophet Elijah)

(The widow of Zarephath, simply, believed whatever was assured by Elijah. She cooked and served Elijah the bread for her family. It was miraculous that neither the flour nor the oil got over and there was, always, oil and flour to cook for the whole family, as per the word of the man up God, assured in the name of the Lord).

Sub Scene Widow's son falls sick

(Everything was going fine and suddenly the son of the woman fell seriously ill).

The widow: (Holds his son's hands and takes his head on her chest and weeps). "O God I don't know what happened to my son his body temperature is very high, he is not opening his eyes and does not eat anything. I am unable to see his condition. He is my only hope for me to live. (beating her breasts and weeping). I don't know why such illness struck my son.

One of her neighbors: He was playing well with his friends till day before, but I wonder how he has suddenly become seriously ill (She embraces the widow to console her. All relatives and friends visit the widow to be with her dying son. As they expected he suddenly dies).

(The widow was pushed to deep agony and was wailing and comes before Elijah with deep lamentations).

The widow: What do you have against me man of God? Did you come to remind me of my sin and to kill my son?

Elijah: (Very much moved by in agony) Give me your son. (He takes her son to the upper room where he is staying. He lays him on his bed. Then he cries out to the loudly Lord). O Lord my God have you brought tragedy also upon this widow, I am staying with by causing her son to die? (Then Elijah stretches himself on the boy three times and every time he cries to the Lord. "O Lord my God let this boy's life return to him").

(The most compassionate God hears the heart broken cry from his servant Elijah and responds so, the soul of the boy returns to the boy. Elijah thanking his faithful God in his heart and soul, carries the boy downstairs. He hands over the child to the grieving mother).

Elijah: (Reflecting the happiness and gratitude to God). Look your son is alive.

(The unbelievable woman receives her child kisses him with tears rolling down her eyes. She recognizes the great miracle. Even the people gathered to share her grief are shocked to find the dead child alive now. They too, acknowledge this miracle and cry with joy and share the happiness of the widow).

The woman: (With her heart and soul overflowing with joy and gratitude, turns to Elijah). Now I know that you are a man of God and that the word of the Lord from your mouth is true. (She kneels raising both hands towards heaven to thank the Lord. The people around her also do the same acknowledging the statement of the woman).

The people in Chorus: Oh, this is a great miracle the dead boy has come to life. Surely the one who brought him to life is a man of God and his God is the true God. We have to bow down and praise that great God of this man of God.

(They all embrace the son of the widow, one by one, and later celebrate the miracle).

Scene 5

Disturbed Ahab and Furious Jezebel

At the royal court King Ahab and Queen Jezebel are in completely demoralized state having no life in their faces. It is so with all those in that royal court. Two spies enter the court and greet the king.

Ahab: What report you have brought? I don't think anything good to hear.

Spy Leader: Your Majesty, I have brought some shocking intelligence report.

Ahab: Nothing will shock me, go ahead with your report.

Spy Leader: Your Majesty the shocking report is that now the people who are originally the Israelites worshipper of Jehovah started believing whatever was said by Elijah as true and the message was from their true God Jehovah. Your Majesty am reading out the report sent to you by our Spy Chief, "The *earth is parched as if with fire the scorching heat of the sun destroys the surviving vegetation, streams dry up and lowing herds and bleating flocks wander in distress. Once flourishing fields have become like burning desert sands, a desolate waste, the groves dedicated to idol worship are leafless. The forest trees afford no more shade. The air is dry and suffocating, dust storms blind* *the eyes and stop the breath. Once prosperous cities and villages have become places of mourning. Hunger and thirst are telling upon man and beast with fearful mortality. Famine with all its horrors comes closer and still closer. This is the end of the report your Majesty, Now the people stopped worshipping Baal and they are secretly worshipping their God Jehovah and praying for rain.*

Visuals of secret worship by Israelites

Jezebel (In a furious tone). "Is it so" Take our troops and kill all those secret worshippers of Jehovah, destroy their places of worship. Do not spare them. In our country no one will worship other gods except our god Baal and goddess Ashtoreth. And send our troops to arrest all the prophets of Jehovah, none of them should be spared, bring them to kill before the altar of our god Baal.

Your Majesty all these troubles are caused by that mad man Elijah. Our troops and intelligence teams should visit every nation on the earth to unearth that man Elijah. Then only can we find a solution for this prevailing famine and the people deserting Baal and going back to Jehovah otherwise everything will become too late. Our country and people will reach a point of no return. Your Majesty, please give these special orders to kill all the prophets of Jehovah and to look for Elijah.

King Ahab: I agree with the queen; I approve her plan of action to kill all the prophets of Jehovah and to look for Elijah from every nation and to bring him before me. I am instituting a most diligent search out for the hiding place of Elijah into the surrounding nations, far and near. I am sending search parties to trace out the man whom I hate and fear. He has created such anxiety therefore; I am seeking report from every kingdom and nation to reply with an oath that they know nothing about the whereabouts of the prophet.

Scene 6

Sharing Session of Rabbis at Gilgal

School of prophets at Gilgal. Chief rabbis from Bethel and Jericho with senior students assemble to share the events rapidly taking place and the spiritual conditions of the Israelites.

Chief Rabbi of Gilgal: I greet you all in the name of the Lord. I thank you all for taking the pain to travel from different destinations despite the dangers waiting for the worshippers of Jehovah under the rule of King Ahab and his wicked wife Jezebel. I request and welcome the Chief Rabbi of Bethel to begin this session of sharing (He bows down towards Rabbi of Jericho as sign of invitation).

Chief Rabbi of Bethel: (Bowing down to everyone). Thank you for this invitation to begin our session. To begin with the apostasy prevailing in Ahab's rule is the result of many years of evil. Step by step, year after year, Israel has been departing from the right way. During the wilderness, God assured them a country where they would never suffer for lack of rain. It is a land of hills and valleys and the drinking water from heaven through rain a land which the Lord cares for and the eyes of the Lord always upon it from the beginning of the year even unto the end of the year.

But the foolish and irresponsible people of Israel from generation after generation refused to make straight paths for their feet and at last the great majority of the people yielded themselves to the leadership and the powers of darkness.

In other words, the devil and his worshippers through various rituals including human sacrifice and deliberately indulging in immoral sex please the evil one and his elements through these long years of drought and famine. There are wide spread agonizing news about Jezebel who managed to kill all the prophets of the Lord, our true God Jehovah.

I would like to add latest information. There are some secret rumors originating from the palace staff, the common people, some of them may be loose talkers from uncultured minds and imaginations but these rumors are secretly a float. They have a question, why is King Ahab submitting to all the demands of his wife Jezebel, including the killing of the prophets of Jehovah? And allowing the King to accept the worship of Baal as national religion? They say that Ahab has suddenly become a religious person, a fanatic a maniac, merciless killer after his marriage with Jezebel. These people say if he is a real man like one of us, he would have questioned his wife. When she wanted to murder all the prophets of Jehovah or he would have objected the construction of Baal temple in the capital. But he is allowing his wife Jezebel to carry on with her evil designs against Jehovah and his people. His marriage was arranged to maintain the tradition of the royal family. But he is not behaving like a man in controlling his wife but always submissive to that wicked woman. Like a henpecked husband, he behaves like a ferocious animal deceptive and a master liar embodiment of Satan the devil, ruthless maniac killer.

Jezebel is fully utilizing the weakness of Ahab and places all her demands with single intention to wipe out the God of Israel from the hearts and minds of the people and to make Baal as the only god of Israel and the pure heathen worship of Satan to become the national religion of Israel. Therefore, she went on with her massacre of all the prophets of Jehovah and the worshippers of Jehovah.

Chief Rabbi of Gilgal: (Raises his hand and continues). I must add here some information about Jezebel. Jezebel is a vivacious beauty and to promote Baal worship she is allowing free sex and declaring debauchery not a sin. Jezebel considers such debauchery and sex offences as honour to Ashtoreth like rituals to please the sex god. The public and the palace officials know about the practice of sexually immoral acts at high places but afraid of their own lives. Therefore, they do not discuss about sexual adventures of people in power like Jezebel directly or indirectly. She is encouraging sexual orgies of men and women in Israel. What else can we expect from a woman of her background? Jezebel greatly influenced the worship of Baal and Ashtoreth declaring them as national gods. May God intervene to save Israel from total moral collapse.

Chief Rabbi of Bethel: (Raises his hand and continues the discussion). Here is some fantastic news (laughs).

Jezebel herself is a seductress and used tricks to entice the Israelites with lusty women with their soul corrupting vivacious flesh to corrupt the Israelites (visuals to be shown) to denounce their religion and customs which were so carefully taught by the prophets and teachers of God for so many centuries. But Israelites have turned totally blind and unable to see the difference between Yahweh the true God and the god Baal, the fake god of Ahab introduced by Jezebel with their ruling power in hands.

The latest and saddest are the worshippers of true God Yahweh have become minority and the Baal worshippers have become majority in Israel. It has become common to see the majority harassing and persecuting the minority with the support of the ruler in Ahab enslaved to Queen Jezebel. The true believers have lost the freedom to worship their true God openly or to follow their customs and traditions rather they practice their religion secretly sometimes from the mountain sides or from the caves and secluded places (Visuals to be shown).

Queen Jezebel's only mission has become to eliminate Yahweh worship from the map of the world.

Chief Rabbi of Gilgal: Even during the wilderness the mixed multitude that came up with the Israelites from Egypt were a source of continual temptation and trouble. They professed to have renounced idolatry and to worship the true God, but their early education and training had moulded their habits and their character. Therefore, they were corrupt with idolatry and with irreverence for God. They leavened the Israelites camp with their idolatrous practices and disobedience to God by not following the Law. There is only superficial information in circulation on moral decadence, but in-depth facts are disturbing and raises doubts whether the people of God would turn to their true God with repentance.

Women have no freedom to walk freely in the streets to buy any household items. There are lusty men waiting to abduct them for gang rape in secluded places even older women are not spared from such sexual assaults. The most horrible news is about murders after rapes to bury the crimes.

Chief Rabbi of Jericho: I am presenting some unnatural news. There is news about women who live with three to four men in the same house to quench their sexual orgies and women kill their husbands even their children for their sexual orgies. Also there are men living with men practicing homosexuality and women living with women practicing lesbianism.

Jezebel, the Queen had declared such of these abnormal and unnatural sexual acts are more pleasing to their fertility and sex gods Baal and Ashtoreth. The temples of Baal and Ashtoreth are carved with unnatural sex acts such as women having sex with animals and single women having sex with multiple partners. All these demoralizing decorations in their temples have convinced the converts to Baalism not to consider any of these sins as sin at all, but natural to human beings for the followers of Baal and Ashtoreth. Yahweh gave the message through all the prophets that Israel should be kept as a pure nation in every respect to guide all the nations and people on earth, but the people did not follow the stern messages of the prophets.

Chief Rabbi of Gilgal: It is horrible to imagine the moral collapse of the Israelites due to the influence of Satan the devil through King Ahab and his wife Queen Jezebel. But I am continuously having prophetic visions. All these rebellion and disobedience to worship the true God and all the sex crimes, sexual immoral life, murders connected with lust and wealth, unimaginable sexual orientations all will go away from Israel due to the tremendous efforts of the future prophets of God who would be sent to reform Israel and once again to worship the true God Jehovah and to follow all his commandments to maintain purity in the society. Israel will remain as a unique nation created by God as per his original plan but, all these filths of sins, unimaginable sex crimes, greed for wealth, division between the worshipper of the true God and the people of the devil as minority and majority respectively. This will totally disappear from Israel. Satan will carry destructive forces of evils crimes, violence, greed for wealth, murders due to sex and wealth and assault by the so called majority. The devil worshippers upon the minority the worshippers of true God will all shift to some other region to make it the final base to corrupt the whole world. That region would be dreaded as most dangerous. Morally a wicked region both the rulers and the citizens will be liars, corrupt, greedy, violent and would be widely known as more dangerous.

So, the devil would make this region as his final headquarters. However, even in this region there will be a minority of worshippers of the true God who will raise their hands towards heaven begging the Lord God to save the people of this region from destruction due to their enslavement to sin and Satan.

God is merciful because of this small population of true worshippers therefore he is patient and bearing with the sinful people of this degraded region. I am unable to pinpoint the region because the visions disappear on that point of identification of that region only time will expose it.

A senior student (Raises his hand and continues). I get some strange imaginations. I get into a peculiar thought that God created the insurmountable mountains, vast deserts, forests which cannot be crossed by humans and oceans beyond human power to cross. May be this is to keep the people or the human races separate, not to allow them to mix which may finally bring no good, but great disasters to destroy the souls of people and their very physical existence. Therefore, the Lord had kept the tree of knowledge in the garden of Eden with clear instructions to Adam and Eve to keep away from that tree.

Senior Rabbi of Jericho: No, no, this is an extreme thought. (All those gathered laugh to approve the objection).

No one can reason out the purpose behind every creative work of God. God has created everything and every human being with a purpose. It would take a life time to understand the mysteries of God. Our only duty with devotion is to walk in his ways to keep his statutes his commandments and his judgments and testimonies that his people should be the light of the world. Therefore, he caused the chosen nation to occupy a strategic position among the nations of earth. The prophets with their suffering made distress call for repentance a divine interposition to save them from taking the fatal step beyond the boundary of heaven's forgiveness. He was helping them to recover their lost faith turning away from the sins that had brought upon them the chastening hand of the Almighty and turning to the Lord with full purpose of heart.

Chief Rabbi from Gilgal: I would say Yahweh from the time of Adam and Eve, Moses and David and with all his prophets and Kings labored with the people to establish a separate nation to become the light of the other nations of the world. To guide them to worship the Only One God the true God Yahweh to establish truth, justice and righteousness in their nation. But alas! due to the weak and wicked Kings, Umri and Ahab, Jezebel came like a whirl wind and took away the nation which was worshipping the true God but to replace with counterfeit Canaanite gods in Baal and Ashtoreth. Jezebel had not sweated there was no need for it she could simply take away because of

Ahab the most corrupt king within no time to convert Israelites as Baal worshippers.

Chief Rabbi of Bethel: I would like to say one thing is very clear that Prophet Elijah's voice is the one crying in the wilderness to rebuke Israel's sins and press back the tide of evil. Unbelief was fast separating the chosen nation from the source of their strength.

Elijah was overwhelmed with sorrow. He is longing to see them brought to repentance before they should go to such lengths in evil doing as to provoke the Lord to destroy them utterly. The worshippers of Baal claimed that the treasures of heaven, the dew and the rain came not from Jehovah therefore until they turn to God with repentance and acknowledge him as the source of all blessing there should fall upon the land neither dew nor rain.

Elijah would make Ahab know who is the true God? Baal or the God of Israel. Creator and Controller of everything including the rain and dew. Let us hope the people get the true light.

Scene 7

Prophet Elijah and Ahab

Visuals of slaughter of Prophets can be added.

Elijah is mourning for the slaughter of the prophets by Ahab and his wife Jezebel. He is in worn out, discouraged in soul. That time the word of the Lord comes to Elijah.

Voice of God: Go show thyself unto Ahab and I will send rain upon the earth.

(Elijah bows down and touches his forehead on the ground as a sign of accepting the command of God and immediately prepares to move).

Sub scene - Obadiah

(Meantime in the royal court-Ahab calls for Obadiah, the Governor of his house and palace. Obadiah presents himself before the King).

Ahab: Obadiah the famine situation has gone out of control there is no ray of hope for rain, the cattle are dying without fodder and left with charred vegetation due to the burning sun. My own home condition is totally famine stricken. I thought of going in search of some vegetation for the cattle and possibility of finding water.

Obadiah: Yes, your Majesty it is a good idea.

Ahab: Well you go in one direction and I will go in another direction, so one of us may find some relief from some corner. You go to all the springs and the valleys. May be we can find some grass to keep the horses and mules alive so we will not have to kill any of our animals.

(So, they divided the land and the routes to cover, Ahab going in one direction and Obadiah in another. As Obadiah is walking along, Elijah meets him. Obadiah recognizes him and bows down to the ground in obeisance).

Obadiah: (With astonishment and joy). Is it really you, my lord Elijah?

Elijah: (Showing his paternal affection). Yes, go tell your master Elijah is here.

Obadiah (greatly shocked and with fear). What have I done wrong that you are handing your servant over to Ahab to be put to death? As surely as the Lord your God lives there is not a nation or kingdom where my master has not sent someone to look for you. And whenever a nation or kingdom claimed you were not there, he made them swear that they could not find you. But now you tell me to go to my master and say, 'Elijah is here 'I don't know where the Spirit of the Lord may carry you when I leave you. If I go and tell Ahab and if he does not find you, he will kill me. Yet I your servant has worshipped the Lord since my youth. Haven't you heard, my Lord what I did while Jezebel was killing the prophets of the Lord? I hid hundreds of Lord's prophets in two caves, fifty in each and supplied food and water. And now you tell me to go to my master and say, 'Elijah is here he will kill me.'

Elijah: (After listening with deep compassion and concern). As the Lord Almighty lives whom I serve I will surely present myself to Ahab today.

(Obadiah assured of Elijah's determination to appear before Ahab he hurries to meet Ahab and finds him).

Obadiah: (Bows down to the king Ahab and with fear utters). Elijah is here.

Ahab: (Astonished, feared, and confused now the man who was sought all through the nations and kingdoms is here. Ahab is murmuring in a very low voice). By meeting Elijah hope there will be no danger to my life. Has he come to utter one more woe against Israel? Better to go with a body guard for self-protection.

(Ahab walks towards Elijah with passion of hatred but feeling powerless before the man of God. Elijah is waiting without any tensions nor reverence for his Majesty).

Ahab :(in faltering words). Is that you the troubler of Israel?

Elijah: (In a clear and bold voice) I have not made trouble for Israel. But you and your father's family have. You have abandoned the Lord's commands and followed Baalism (in a commanding voice).

Now summon the people from all over Israel to meet me on Mount Carmel. And bring the four hundred and fifty prophets of Baal and the four hundred prophets of Asherah who eat at Jezebel's table. Let the true God of Israel reveal himself on Mount Carmel as the only God and there is no other God other than him.

(King Ahab obeys at once, as if the prophet is the monarch, and himself as his subject).

Ahab: (Orders his court officials). Send messengers to entire nation summoning all the people and the all the prophets of Baal and Asherah to gather at Mount Carmel to meet prophet Elijah. (The messengers disperse to make the announcement of the king, to the entire nation - Israel).

Scene 8

Mount Carmel

Mount Carmel's beauty languished under a withering curse. The altars erected to the worship of Baal and Ashtoreth stood now in leafless groves. On the summit of one of the highest ridges, in sharp contrast in these was the broken - down altar of Jehovah. Carmel overlooked a wide expanse of country; its heights were visible from many parts of the kingdom of Israel. Elijah chooses the elevated spot as the most conspicuous place for the display of God's power and for the vindication of the honour of his name. The people of Israel in eager expectancy gather near the top of the mountain. Their faces reflect anxiety to get over the three years famine coupled with extreme sufferings. Jezebel's prophets arch up in imposing array. In regal pomp, the king appears and takes his position as the head of the prophets of Baal and Ashtoreth.

Elijah: (Unashamed, not terrified, Elijah stands before the multitude, fully aware of his commission to execute. His countenance is lighted with an awful solemnity. Looking first upon the broken-down altar of Jehovah and then upon the multitude, Elijah cries out in clear trumpet like tones). How long will you waver between two opinions? If the Lord is God follow him but if Baal is god follow him.

(There is dead silence among the multitudes, simply bowing down their heads accepting their ignorance on that question. While Israelites on Mount Carmel doubt and hesitate, Elijah breaks the silence).

Elijah: I am the only one of the Lord's prophets left but Baal has four hundred and fifty prophets. Get two bulls for us, let them choose one for themselves and cut them into pieces and put it on the wood, but not set fire to it. I will prepare the other bull and put it on the wood, but not set fire to it. Then you call on the name of your god and I will call on the name of the Lord. The god who answers by fire he is God.

(There comes a reply in chorus from the multitude, with happy faces).

The people: What you say is good.

One voice from the multitudes: Yes, it must be proved who is the real god whether the old God Jehovah or the new god lord Baal to know who the controller of rain is.

Elijah: (On hearing the voice of the people, turns to the prophets of Baal).

Choose one of the bulls and prepare it first since there are so many of you. Call on the name of your god but do not light the fire.

(The battalion of prophets of Baal and Ashtoreth chose one bull and prepare it to place on the altar of Baal. Outwardly they look bold, but inwardly struck with fear they surround the altar and begin their incantations raising their hands and voices towards the idol of Baal, closer to the altar).

Prophets of Baal: O Baal hear us (Their shrill cries echo and reecho through the forests and the surrounding heights. They repeat the same plea).

Prophets of Baal: O Baal hear us.

Prophets of Baal: O Baal hear us.

This goes on for hours and at break time the drummers consume liquor to recharge themselves to beat that gigantic drum. The sound from the drums echo through mountains and the villages below Mount Carmel. Babies in the cradles wake up, frightened and cry. The people fear that they may turn deaf by the sound of the elephant sized drums.

Visuals of Drumming

All the prophets of Baal and Ashtoreth gather around their altar, where the dressed animal flesh is waiting for Baal to consume it by fire. They start leaping, writhing, screaming and tearing their hair. Some of them cutting their own flesh to draw the attention of their god Baal. However, since all of them know that Baal has neither life nor power to demonstrate by fire, to consume the animal flesh they plan to find out dubious means to create some fire around the altar to cheat the people that Baal had sent the fire. Some prophets whisper, to pass their message through air.

Prophets: O Baal please help us we are ready to give you any amount of gold and silver. Look we have brought hundred bagsful of silver and gold we are ready to give you more but please hear us.

Another prophet (whispers): Baal we know that you have a weakness for beautiful women. Please help us as a reward we will arrange most beautiful women to come around you naked in your temple and dance to satisfy your lust.

Sub Scene

At Baal's temple built by Ahab

(The prophets of Baal send young and beautiful women, semi naked or fully naked, to dance before the idol of Baal in his temple). Some bring bulls and force them to stand in queue.

Devotees of Baal: O Baal all these bulls are for you to slaughter them the moment you send fire to consume the animal flesh offered on your altar on Mount Carmel. Please hurry up do not delay.

(One of their prophets is a poet he starts reciting most beautiful poem in honour of Baal the people are thrilled by the beautiful poem).

Poetic prophet: (recites a poem).

"The *head of our god Baal resembles the rising sun in the east*

Oh, his handsome face resembles the sunset throwing beauties in west

Baal's arms are like the mountain ranges descending to embrace lusty women

His legs are like teak forests to satisfy the unquenchable lusts of women

His eyes are like red sky, sexy with unbeatable stamina known to Ashtoreth

When Baal kisses Ashtoreth…the rain and dew fall on earth from their hot lips

When Baal embraces his sweet heart Ashtoreth...streams flow from their hips

Worshippers of Baal and Ashtoreth men and women drink and swim in liquor

Running like rivers from the feet of Baal dance with sexual mirth till eternity."

Sub Scene

Back to Mount Carmel

(When the prophets of Baal were dancing and going closer to the altar, Elijah is watching every moment of these dubious prophets, so they do not find any dubious means to set fire on the animal flesh. Some of them are conducting rituals of sacrificing birds and animals and burning them in the pit near the altar. Elijah goes closer to check that they are not transferring any fire from the pits where they are busy conducting various rituals. The smoke from the pits raise hovering voices around the altar of Baal, where the flesh offering is waiting for fire to consume. Some of the worshippers of Baal are cheering up, on seeing the smoke but are severely dejected).

One prophet: (with blood dripping from his face and a vessel in hand): Baal, see I have killed my only son to please you I am going to pour out his blood on your idol in the temple please hear us. Baal please hear us see the fresh blood of my only son slaughtered before your idol to please you.

(Visuals)

(They are carrying on their senseless and barbaric ceremonies to draw the attention of their god Baal. Morning is over, and noon time set in. Elijah plans to mock them to bring shame to the prophets and sense to the people).

Elijah: (mockingly). Shout louder, surely he is a god! Perhaps he is deep in thought or busy travelling. Maybe he is sleeping and must be awakened.

One voice: (From the frustrated and angry crowd). Baal may be having sex with Ashtoreth so do not want to be disturbed(laughs).

Another voice: (whispers). No one may be having homosexual pleasure with his worshippers.

(The disappointed and depressed prophets shout and finding no answer they start cutting their own bodies part by part as per their custom They smear their own blood on their faces and foreheads. They all resemble blood-soaked animals in distress movements. The time for offering at the altar is over there is no answer from Baal and evening draws on. The prophets of Baal are weary, faint, confused, finally they cease their efforts. Their shrieks and curses no longer resound over Carmel. In despair they retire from the contest. Their guilt reflects on their faces for misguiding the people all these years, for idol worship and devil worship. Most of them have spent their whole lives in such deceit, deceiving themselves and deceiving ordinary people. More than the prophets, the people are the dejected lot, with agony stocked on their faces. Their great anxiety is on, when to get water if Baal is not the rain god. They are completely demoralized).

One prophet of Baal: (Totally frustrated, whole body soaked with blood of self-inflictions, he becomes very angry on Baal and abuses). You lazy, impotent, eunuch. Baal you have cheated us. You have fooled us. Now we understand that you are nothing, but an idol made of mud and stone, you put us to shame before the people. Wait tomorrow, I will bring my dogs to piss on your face in your temple. Yes, Baal I am not going to leave you.

One voice from the crowd: We want rain so we can get food and water. It is so horrible to see our prophets. They resemble wild animals after a big fight, blood oozing out from all over their bodies from their torn flesh. They are left with no strength to say anything. They are not losers, after all they eat at the table of Queen Jezebel, but we the people are the worst sufferers. Not seen the rain or streams for more than three years. Such a thing never happened when we were worshipping Jehovah. All these curses fell upon us only after the arrival of Jezebel as Queen of our King Ahab.

A loud voice from the crowd: Our eyes are opened now. We understand Jehovah has restrained Satan. Satan would have gladly sent the lightning to kindle their sacrifice and not all the enemy's devices can convey one spark to Baal's altar. The exhibition of demonism by Baal's prophets have failed. Now our redemption is in the efforts of Elijah the prophet. We must wait and see the actions of Elijah. More than us we can see the devastated prophets of Baal more keenly watching Elijah and the hour of evening sacrifice is nearing.

Elijah :(Elijah is sure of his time to demonstrate the power of the True God. Looking at the people sympathetically). "Come here to me..." The people felt it as a command from some unknown space they hurried moving in trembling to go nearer to Elijah. Elijah went nearer to the Lord's altar, in a ruined condition. He takes twelve stones, one for each of the tribes descended from Jacob. He builds an altar in the name of the Lord. Further, he digs a trench around the altar large enough to hold two seeds of seed. Then he arranges the wood and after that he offers the bull sacrifice and he lay it flesh on the wood.

Elijah: (At this point he asks the people). Fill four large jars of water and pour it on the meat and on the wood. (The people follow his instructions).

Elijah: Do it again. (The people bring four large jars of water and pour it on the offering and on the wood).

Elijah: Do it a third time. (The people follow his instructions with surprise and fear on their faces. And the water runs around the altar and fills the trenches also. The followers of Baal are watching the calm and devout actions of prophet Elijah and same time comparing the devilish sounds and actions of their prophets to move Baal into action, to consume the offering. The calm demeanor of the prophet stands out in sharp contrast with the fanatical, senseless frenzy of the followers of Baal).

Elijah: (At the time of sacrifice. The prophet steps forward and prays). O Lord, God of Abraham, Isaac and Israel, let it be known today that you are God in Israel and that I am your servant and have done all these things at your command. Hear me O Lord, please hear me that these people may know that thou art the Lord God and thou hast turned their hearts back again.

(No sooner is the prayer of Elijah ended, that flames of fire, like brilliant flashes of lightning descend from heaven upon the altar, consuming the sacrifice, licking up the water in the trench and consuming even the stones of the altar. The brilliancy and blaze illumine the mountain and dazzles the eyes of the multitude. In the valley below, where many are watching in anxious suspense, the movements of those above, the descent of fire is clearly seen, and all are amazed at the sight. It resembles the pillar of fire, which at the Red Sea separated the children of Israel from the Egyptian host. The people on the mount prostrate themselves in awe before the unseen God. They dare not continue to look upon the heaven-sent fire. They fear that they themselves will be consumed and convicted of their duty to acknowledge the God of Elijah as the God of their fathers, to whom they owe allegiance, they cry out together, with one voice).

The people: The Lord, he is the God the Lord he is the God. (The cry resounds over the mountain and echoes in the plains below).

Elijah: (With a clear and emotional commanding tone, as though he got the command from the Lord). Seize the prophets of Baal. Don't let anyone get away.

(The multitudes were already frustrated, for being let down by Baal. They realize that these prophets of Baal were the instruments of the devil, who misguided them from the true God and Lord Jehovah. So, they run towards the prophets of Baal, to capture them as per the command of prophet Elijah to bring them to Kishon Valley).

The prophets of Baal had neither physical strength nor moral strength to defend themselves or stamina to run away due to their strain and pain and loss of blood while praying to Baal to hear them: so, have lost all strength. King Ahab is also shocked. Whatever happened was true and seen or witnessed by him but there was numbness in his soul and body. He is unable to speak or nothing to speak. He is standing like a beaten down man in a battle.

The Chief prophet of Baal: (with broken heart, utters audible to his fellow prophets):

We deserve to be killed by prophet Elijah. All through our life we have been deceiving the people in the name of Baal who is an idol used by the devil to dishonor the true God of Elijah. We have no merit to lifestyle, there is no repentance in us. It may be because at the heart of us we are still worshippers of Baal let Elijah do with us whatever his Lord commands him to do.

(Visuals)

(The multitudes which ran to capture them found the whole lot of prophets of Baal, in demoralized silent state. They bring them to the Kishon Valley. The day is closing with darkness slowly gripping. Elijah stands there as a warrior from heaven. His command is carried out. The prophets of Baal are slaughtered without any mercy, till the last one was killed. And there before the close of the day that marked the beginning of decided reform, the ministers of Baal were slain. Not one is permitted to live).

One of the witnesses from Carmel to Kishon Valley: Now the way is cleared for prophet Elijah with the slaying of the prophets of Baal. The way is opened to carry forward a mighty spiritual reformation among the ten tribes of the Northern kingdom. Elijah has set before the people their apostasy; he calls up on them to humble their hearts and turn to the Lord. The judgment of heaven had been executed, the people now confess their sins and acknowledge the God of their fathers as the living God and now the curse of heaven will be withdrawn and the temporal blessing of life to be renewed. The land will be refreshed with rain. Elijah did whatever was commanded by God to do. Now he is standing to witness the heavy rain assured by the Lord, although there is no sign of rain.

Elijah: (Turning to Ahab and in crystal clear voice). Get thee up eat and drink for there is a sound of abundance of rain.

(Elijah climbs to the top of Mount Carmel, putting his face between his knees, he prays for rain and for forgiveness of

Israelites, who have come back, after witnessing the miraculous happenings at Mount Carmel. After some time, he calls the servant).

Elijah: Go and look towards the sea.

Servant: (After his watch on Mediterranean Sea). There is nothing there.

Elijah: (Praying more earnestly he calls back the servant). Go and look towards the sea.

Servant: (After finishing his watch on the sea he returns to Elijah). There is nothing there.

Elijah (Continues praying without any sign of discouragement in his face. Calls back the servant). Go and look towards the sea

Servant: (Comes back). There is nothing there.

Elijah: (After some time again sends the servant). Go and look towards the sea.

Servant: (Losing hope to find anything at the same time having sympathy on Elijah to give the negative reply). There is nothing there.

Elijah: (Without any anxiety in his face). Go and look towards the sea.

Servant: (Walks without any hope to find anything and after his watch comes back to say). There is nothing there.

Elijah: (Spends little more time pleading to the Lord and calls back the servant) Go and look towards the sea.

Servant: (With a broken spirit and loss of faith). There is nothing there.

Elijah: (Untiringly, ordering the servant). Go and look towards the sea.

Servant: (He looks at the sea and finds a little cloud so comes running to Elijah to deliver this different message, breathing heavily) Behold there arises a little cloud out of the sea like a man's hand. After delivering this message he watches eagerly the face of his master Elijah.

Elijah: (To his servant). Go and tell Ahab, Hitch up your chariot and go down before the rain stops you.

Sub Scene: The Great Run

(A mighty show of God's power on prophet Elijah to be appropriately filmed in the pattern of the Film Benhur and First Great Run, by Elijah).

As Ahab prepares for his descent. It came to pass in the meanwhile, that the heaven becomes black with clouds and wind, and there comes a great rain. Elijah the prophet of God, still acknowledges Ahab as Israel's king and as an act of honour, strengthened by the power of God, tucking his coat into his belt, he runs before the royal chariot, guiding the King to the entrance of the city of Jezreel, a distance of 17 miles, only God's power can enable such run competing the chariot of the king, amidst heavy rain full of thunders and lightning.

(Moments of speechless scenes of King Ahab and Prophet Elijah).

At the entrance of the palace, Ahab and Elijah stand, may be the perspiring prophet and the mystery struck the King. King Ahab is standing like an imbalanced man, who had witnessed too many miracles, at a stretch, starting from Mount Carmel to his Royal palace gate. Now, he witnessed the prowess of Elijah, who ran before his chariot to guide him to reach safely the gate of his palace.

Ahab is stormed with several emotions, even, may be to kneel before the prophet for all the miracles that he has done and for the very kind act of reaching him to his palace, when facing great perils in that stormy rain. He stands speechless. On the other side, within no time Elijah leaves Ahab without saying anything, on finishing his mission to see Ahab had reached his palace. Jezreel is a summer palace which might have been the residence of Ahab and the royal family during the past three years, due to the burning sun and parching heat without rain. Elijah walks out of the palace gate,wraps himself to his mantle and lies down on the bare earth to sleep.

King Ahab hurries to meet Queen Jezebel to tell her every miraculous event that he had witnessed. In fact, the Queen was anxiously waiting for Ahab in her chamber.

Ahab: (Rushing inside Jezebel's chamber). Jezebel, I rushed from Mount Carmel riding my chariot amidst the thunderous rain fallen on our nation after three years of famine and drought. I had seen miracle after miracle all performed by prophet Elijah on the Mount Carmel.

Jezebel: What? Miracles by Elijah! Are you in your senses?

Ahab: Yes, I am very much in my senses rather my senses have woken up after a long stupid slumber.

Jezebel: (In an irritated voice). I don't understand anything you say.

Ahab: Yes, you won't understand because all miracles were performed by Elijah whom you hate and plan to kill. But he has proved himself as a man of God to the entire nation in a single day. The first test was challenging your prophets. All prophets of Baal pray to Baal to consume the bull meat on the altar through fire from heaven. Prophets of Baal failed miserably despite their desperate cries and prayers to Baal tearing their own flesh and streaming their own blood. But Baal did not respond. Then prophet Elijah came on the scene he repaired the altar of Jehovah placed the meat at the altar and poured water, he then filled the trenches around the altar with water. Then he prayed to his God Jehovah to accept his sacrifice by sending fire from heaven. A miracle took place. Heavenly fire came down and not only consumed the bull's meat, but also the altar stones and dried up the water stored near the altar. The next moment there were cries from the people praising their Lord Jehovah and begging him to forgive their sins for worshipping Baal.

Jezebel: (becomes hysteric and shouts crying). O! Baal, our god why did you let us down? Why did you allow that man Elijah to defame you in front of all your worshippers? Why didn't you consume Elijah by sending fire? Oh my god Baal? (Then she turns to Ahab with terribly disturbed face). Then what happened further?

Ahab: (hesitatingly). Elijah commanded the people to catch hold of all the prophets of Baal not sparing even one. Accordingly, they were taken to Kishon Valley and killed and none of the prophets of Baal could escape.

Jezebel: (In a shocked condition beating her breasts). God Baal, how can you allow your prophets to be killed by Elijah. The people converted from Israel faith to Baal's faith what shame and tragedy you have brought upon your faithful worshippers? How do we to rebuild the faith of Baal worship? How could you become inactive in the time of testing on the Mount Carmel and at the Kishon valley? Where your four hundred and fifty prophets slaughtered? (Suddenly she shouts raising her hands upward). I will see Elijah meets the same fate as the prophets of Baal. I want a messenger immediately to deliver my message to Elijah.

(A messenger appears before Jezebel and bows down).

Jezebel: (with highly raised voice dictates the message to be delivered to Elijah). So let the gods do to me and more also if I make not thy life of one of them by tomorrow about this time.
Messenger: Yes, your Majesty our Queen, I will immediately deliver your message to prophet Elijah. (He leaves the Royal Court).

Scene 9

Moses Experience of Elijah at the Mountain Top

Elijah is resting after he left King Ahab. He is hopeful that the miracles and demonstration of Jehovah's divine power on Mount Carmel might have brought repentance in the minds of the King and Queen. More importantly Queen Jezebel may stop influencing the King, which will enable the speedy reformation, the need of the hour. All day on Carmel's height he had toiled without food. Yet when he guided the chariot of Ahab to the gate of Jezreel, his courage was strong, despite the physical strain under which he labored. Such of these positive imaginations rather expectations are flashing in the mind of the over worked wearied prophet. The messenger sent by Jezebel arrives to deliver the message to Prophet Elijah.

Messenger: (Wakes up the prophet from his sleep to deliver the life threatening message). This is the message to you from Queen Jezebel, " So let the gods do to me and more also if I make not thy life as the life of one of them by tomorrow about this time".

(Prophet Elijah's negative and fearful thoughts reflect on his face and body movements! The reaction of the message is, like elevated to the height of Pisgah, and suddenly thrown down to reach the bottom of the valley. He feared that the reformation began on Mount Carmel might not be lasting and depression seized him. Bewildered and in this dark hour his faith and courage forsook him. He woke up from his slumber. The rain was pouring from heavens, and darkness on every side. God had directed his course to a place of refuge from the hatred of Jezebel and the search of Ahab, the prophet now fled for his life. On reaching Beersheba, he left his servant there and went further a day's journey into the wilderness. With Jezebel's threat sounding in his ears and Satan still apparently prevailing through the plotting of this wicked woman, he lost his hold on God. He found himself in a dreary waste, alone. Utterly wearied he sat down to rest under a juniper tree. In his totally disintegrated state, he prayed).

Elijah: (Prays). I have had enough Lord take away my life for I am not better than my ancestors. (Utterly exhausted and he falls asleep).

(Prophet Elijah in disintegrated state). A fugitive, far from the dwelling places of men, his spirits crushed by bitter disappointments, utterly exhausted he falls asleep. As Elijah sleeps, a soft touch and a pleasant voice wakes him up. He stares up in terror, to flee as if the enemy had discovered him. But the pitying face bending over him is not the face of an enemy, but of a friend. God has sent an angel from heaven, with food for his servant).

Angel: (With face, full of love and compassion). Arise and eat, (Elijah finds a cake baked on the coals, and a cruise of water at his head! Elijah eats the cake baked for him; and with the hunger disappeared, again falls asleep).

(Once again, the angel appears beside him, touching the exhausted man with pitying tenderness).

Angel: (The angel says). Arise and eat because the journey is too great for you. (Elijah obliges by eating the refreshment from heaven, offered by God's angel and in the strength of that food- he can journey forty days and forty nights to reach Horeb the mountain of God. There he finds a cave as shelter for him. The weary and discouraged prophet was not left to struggle alone with the powers of darkness, that was pressing upon him).

The Voice of the Lord: What are you doing here Elijah?

Elijah: (Recognizing the voice of God he bows down before the Almighty). I have been very zealous for the Lord God Almighty. The Israelites have rejected your covenant, broken down your altars and put your prophets to death, with sword. I am the only one left now and they are trying to kill me too.

The Voice of the Lord: Go out and stand on the mountain in the presence of the Lord for the Lord is about to pass by. (Elijah's spirit is energized).

Then a great and powerful wind tore the mountains apart and shattered the rocks before the Lord, but the Lord was not in the wind. (This could be the reason why there are lakhs of mountains on the earth where one can find unbelievable sight of big rocks positioned on each other and in some mountains a small rock bearing the weight of a big rock and also the rocks on the top of the mountains in helter and skelter ways, raising the eye brows to see these fantastic appearance of mountains: how these rocks were placed on each other in these mysterious manner). After the wind there was an earthquake, but the Lord was not in the earthquake. After the earthquake came a fire, but the Lord was not in the fire.

And after the fire came a gentle whisper. On hearing it, he pulls his cloak over his face and goes out and stands at the mouth of the cave. God meets his tired servant with the inquiry. Not in mighty manifestations of divine power, but by "a still small voice"; God does not choose to reveal himself to his servant.

The voice of God: What are you doing here Elijah? I sent you to the brook Kerith Ravine and afterward to the widow at Zarephath. I commissioned you to return to Israel and to stand before the idolatrous priests on Carmel. I guided you with strength to guide the chariot of the King to the gate of Jezreel. But who sent you on this hasty flight into the wilderness? What errand have you here?

Elijah: (In bitterness of soul mourned out his complaint). I have been very zealous for the Lord God Almighty. The Israelites have rejected your covenant broken down your altars and put your prophets to death with sword. I am the only one left and now they are trying to kill me too.

Voice of God: (Neither with sympathy for Elijah nor with any displeasure). Go back the way you came and go to the desert of Damascus. When you get there anoint Hazel king over Aram. Also, anoint Jehu son of Nimshi king over Israel and anoint Elisha son of Shamhat from Abel Meholah to succeed you as prophet. Jehu will put to death any one who escapes the sword of Hazel and Elisha will put to death any one who escape the sword of Jehu. Yet I reserved seven thousand in Israel all those knees have not bowed down to Baal and all those mouths have not kissed him.(Prophet Elijah bows down and his whole self is recharged and renewed. He stands still after hearing the voice of God).

Scene 10

Developments
the School of Prophets at Bethel

The mass slaughter of prophets of Baal, at the Kishon Valley on the command of Elijah spreads like wild fire. That reaches the Schools of Prophets at Bethel, Gilgal and Jericho. The Chief Rabbi from Gilgal and Jericho arrive speedily to the School of Bethel, to discuss the latest developments on Mount Carmel. The Rabbis and the students assemble at the auditorium to know more about the facts and the later developments.

Chief Rabbi of Gilgal: (Greets everyone as per their custom). I hurried to meet you all after hearing about the great events that have taken place on Mount Carmel. Prophet Elijah defeated King Ahab and Jezebel and also the worshippers of Baal, by proving our Lord as the True God. We the three senior Rabbis from three school of prophets have decided to have a long session to exchange the facts and experiences that had rapidly taken place due to our prophet Elijah. We intend to share not only the action filled mission of prophet Elijah but the aftermath and the prevailing situation in Israel taking into consideration the future of God's chosen people and the chosen nation.

Chief Rabbi of Bethel: It is a great thing to spend the day together to share. To begin with what happened on Mount Carmel where the Lord with his fire from heaven honored Prophet Elijah by consuming the offering on the altar not even sparing the stones and proved himself as the true God. But the end event was saddening as all the prophets of Baal were slaughtered mercilessly sparing not even one prophet. Was it a revengeful act against Queen Jezebel's killing of hundreds of the prophets of the true God in order to wipe out the worship of Jehovah?

Chief Rabbi of Jericho: I think it not so the Lord would not have waited for such a long time. If he wanted revenge for his prophets by Queen Jezebel he would have done it the very next moment after the slaughter of his prophets. But the Lord had demonstrated his plan for the Chosen people and the Chosen nation. As per his voice from the beginning that the people of God must keep themselves pure and holy by keeping away from the people of heathen nations. The Lord wanted prophet Elijah to carry out killing of all the prophets of Baal not sparing even one because even if one was left, he would have sown the poison of devil worship and idol worship upon the future generation of the people of God. The idol worship featured with witchcraft, sorcery, human sacrifice, greed for money, immoral sex life of debauchery and adultery or free sex, corruption of all kinds from money to positions in public life. So, to say breaking down of all the Ten Commandments, law and decrees of the Lord. The Lord is not happy to kill the people even the wicked people as per our history, but the Lord is very particular that paganism must not mix to invalidate the law of God given through the Prophets of God. This may be the reason why the Lord has ordered prophet Elijah to slaughter all the prophets of Baal not sparing even one. The most merciful God is also a jealous God who does not expect any rival god.

Chief Rabbi of Gilgal: Of course, it is true that no one can rob the honour of our Lord. However, in killing prophets of Baal not sparing even one has another side which is a serious concern of the Lord about the holy and moral life of his Chosen people may be. The devil began his mission of demoralization from the Garden of Eden by misguiding the innocent first man and woman created by God, Adam and Eve. By their one disobedience to God, sin has become a permanent evil in human society. Satan never sleeps, his mission is to misguide God's people and to create enmity between God and his creatures. In Noah's time, sin reached the zenith to the extent that God regretted creating human beings. Their sins have reached heaven's door. They built the Babel Tower to intrude into God's domain and finally God decided to destroy the entire human population as punishment for their disobedience and sins. However, sparing the pious Noah with his plan to re-create the human population and every living creature of that time. That was God's mercy not to destroy everything that he has created. He made this assurance through the rainbow in the sky.

Chief Rabbi from Jericho: Also it may be that the Lord wanted to put an end to the intrusion of satan among the Chosen people through the prophets of Baal, who would have surely revived devil worship with idols like that of Baal and Ashtoreth and many more would have been createby the devil. He is a master liar and an incomparable deceiver whose only work is to create new gods giving them names and making them famous through very interesting stories in poetry form to attract the innocent people targeting the people of God from the chosen nation. His master plan is to introduce innumerable unimaginable sins into the society as revenge against the Satan, a diabolic planner. He will use his evil designs to break all the Ten Commandments of the Lord. He will put new innumerable gods with lots of stories and falsehood to replace the Only One true God Jehovah. Then he will influence and trap the people of God to break every Law of God to establish a most wicked anti-God. Satan centered human society wherein debauchery, killing, stealing, lying, lust for women and properties and over and above stories to divide God's people as rich and poor, high and low, clean and unclean. All such efforts are to defeat Jehovah's plan of redemption of Israelites from paganism and devil worship.

Chief Rabbi of Bethel: To make it clearer to free them, totally, from the practice of slavery and the human rights violations which they learnt in Egypt. The Lord wanted to guide them for their new nation with Law and holy life. But Satan will try to bring slavery among the Israelites with new stories to form a barbaric animal society where there will be no more respect for parents or for the family life human beings roaming like barbaric animals in the society. The kingdom of God on earth and the rule of righteousness in personal life and social relationship of all men and women by obeying the Ten Commandments will be thrown to the air. Justice and righteousness, love for fellow human beings, equality of all people before God, every such spiritual quality will disappear, and instead satanic society will emerge there will be no more peace and love rather terrible violence and blood bath on various divisions caused masterfully by the devil. Perhaps, the Lord may be sure even if a single prophet of Baal was left to escape. He would have been good enough to create once again devil worship which will be followed with a totally debased human society full of sins and crimes.

He will make God's people as unholy people to disconnect the communication between God and his people.

(The audience with fellow teachers and the students of the School of prophet, listen in silence, whatever was poured out from the mind and mouth of the senior Rabbi as though God is speaking through him).

Chief Rabbi of Gilgal: I fully agree with the Chief Rabbis of Jericho and Bethel. Our Lord's main concern has always been the Kingdom of God on earth and the rule of righteousness in the personal life and social relationship of all men and women in a just and peaceful human society which follow the Commandments of God. Satan the Devil will invent counterfeit commandments to nullify God's Ten Commandments to establish the kingdom of Satan the devil on earth and the rule of most unrighteousness in the personal life and social life which would be the essence of Satan tailored human society.

Chief Rabbi of Gilgal: I fully agree with whatever was spoken by the Senior Rabbi of Gilgal. As far as our Lord is concerned his serious formation of a model nation in Israel as highly moral and ethically strong society which should become a guiding society for the heathen nations, or such ideal society should draw the attraction of the whole universe. One God, One Law and One Humanity. Therefore, from the beginning the Lord was warning his Chosen people to keep away from the heathen nations and societies and not to get contaminated to the extent of losing their precious souls for worldly and fleshly pleasures offered by Satan and his people. In other words, the Lord ordered Elijah to kill all the prophets of Baal not sparing even one in order to check the further spread of idol worship or devil worship identified with witchcraft, sorcery, human sacrifice, corruptions, sexually immoral society in other words sinful inhuman society without any moral or spiritual sense.

Chief Rabbi of Bethel: As per the information in float from the palace officials and the common people there is a new culture emerging after the arrival of Jezebel. Women of our country no more following virtues of womanhood such as chastity, loyalty in married life, love for husband and children. Now women are competing with men in the areas of sexual adventures. Jezebel encouraged immoral sex life to please Baal and Ashtoreth. The shocking news is these totally demoralized people of the country are calling this characterless woman Jezebel as their mother just because she allows free prostitution and all types of corruptions in the whole country of Israel. She is loved by the people a woman without any character as their own mother. Now Israel society is "Like mother the characterless citizens - Deceptive and frauds." Nowhere in the world such defamation is made to motherhood, but Jezebel has succeeded to throw off the sanctity of motherhood of the world with her diabolic schemes and loose life. This woman without character or any virtue is highly venerated by the people of Israel by showing love, affection and respect. Women and children are no longer safe to go out of their homes there are incidents of gang rapes. Satan is inspiring the people to commit such unimaginable and unknown sex crimes among our people. After sex crimes the victims are being killed and thrown down into the caves or into the valleys.

Chief Rabbi of Gilgal: I also heard that there is one more culture emerging that is animal worship. The golden calf was the first dishonor shown by the Israelites to our Lord after crossing the Red Sea under the great servant of God Moses. That golden calf was not thrown away once for all with repentance by the

Israelites. But along with golden calf the new faith to worship golden calves as living gods has become a practice. Anyone who harmed calves or killed them for meat were mercilessly killed. The fatted calf and its meat used to be the choice to cook for any celebration. Now that joy is no more anyone who touches the calf to kill them for meat will be lynched to death. For them calves are superior to human beings created by God in his own image. It did not end up with the golden calf after crossing the Red Sea. Now Satan is introducing animal gods to worship even pigs and fishes in the form of idols. Human beings whosoever kills or harms these animals are mercilessly killed so this is a new tendency to value human life as lesser than animals.

Chief Rabbi of Jericho: This is very sad to know. The truth is by breaking the Commandments of the Lord the people of God have become slaves to the devil which has further enslaved them to greed for wealth and covetousness. Further, turning them to sex addiction. Baal's offer of wealth and sexual orgies drew up weak minded worshippers of Jehovah to become Baal worshippers who have become a majority and the worshippers of Jehovah have become the minority among the population of Israel. The worshippers of Jehovah are living in fear, stress and strain. They are being treated as slaves. The Israelites were disobedient and rebeled all the while.

When the Lord was moving out the Israelites with Moses to guide their ways through the Red Sea and the wilderness the Israelites were not satisfied with the manna, the miraculous food from heaven for forty years. They murmured and complained that variety of delicious food in Egypt and even they desired to go back to Egypt breaking away from the exodus. The Lord guided them to give them a nation flowing with honey and milk and to meet the basic needs of everyone in the new nation.

The Lord did not desire anyone to be landless or homeless. He desired all must get everything and live happily and peacefully with each other. More than this all he wanted his people as free citizens in their own country with no more slavery or injustice to fellow citizens. The devil cheated even the minority population with interesting stories and poetry to attract them. Those who did not respond to them were branded as low-class people and those who admired and recited the stories and poetry before the idols were called high-class people within Israel.

Chief Rabbi of Gilgal: I must add some more shocking information. Satan has not stopped his activities here, but he is inspiring the crook and corrupt minds to invent lethal weapons to kill each other. It may be the intention of the devil in the race to invent and possess large scale lethal weapons, wars will break out between nations and the end may be global suicide. In other words, killing all the human beings, created and protected by God. The devil is trying to guide the entire global population for destruction, but this is beyond the grasp of human minds.

Senior Teacher from Jericho: I would point out that there are lessons to be learnt from prophet Elijah's experience during these days of discouragement and apparent defeat. There are many lessons to be drawn. Lessons invaluable to the servants of God in the ages to come. The apostasy prevailing today would further overspread in Israel during the ages. The great error in the exaltation of the human above the divine in the praise of popular leaders in the worship of mammon and in the placing of the teachings of science above the truths of revelation multitudes would follow new Baals. Doubt and unbelief are exercising their baleful influence over the mind and heart and many would be substituting for the oracles of God the theories of men. It is publicly taught that human race has reached a time when human reason would be exalted above the teachings of the Word. The Law of God. The divine standard of righteousness would be declared to no effect. The enemy of all the truth is working with deceptive powers to cause men and women to place human institutions without God. And to ignore everything ordained by God for the happiness and salvation of humankind.

Chief Rabbi of Bethel: Very tough indeed but truth and revelation for us from God Almighty. Whatever happened on Mount Carmel would remain an eternal lesson for the whole humankind until eternity. The Lord heard the prayers of his faithful servant Elijah. The fire came down from heaven and consumed the offer on the altar not sparing even the altar and stones and then again, he obliged Elijah when he prayed for rain from the top of Mount Carmel. The miracle also happened in Israel when it rained after three years with lightning and thunders. The third miracle, the Great Run ever recorded obeying the command of Lord Elijah was empowered by God to run before the chariot of King Ahab competing with the horses from Mount Carmel to Jezreel the summer palace to guide him to reach the palace. That great run of seventeen miles was not performed on the fair and good road meant for the race but from the terrains of Mount Carmel amidst stormy rain, thunders and lightning. Elijah did that seventeen miles run without a break anywhere until he reached the gate of palace at Jezreel's fire, the rain and finally the Great Run all were divinely ordained to remind the people of God that God Almighty can do such miracles through anyone who is loyal to him.

Chief Rabbi of Gilgal: It is true but at the same time there was a lesson for Elijah too. Elijah had thought that he alone in Israel was a worshipper of the true God. But he who reads the hearts of all revealed to the prophet that there were many others who through the long years of apostasy had remained true to him. God said to Elijah, "I have left me seven thousand in Israel all the knees which have not bowed unto Baal and every mouth which hath not kissed him." Much depends on the unceasing activity of those who are true and loyal and for this reason, Satan puts forth every possible effort to thwart the divine purpose to be wrought out through the obedient. He causes some to lose sight of their high and holy mission and become satisfied with the pleasures of this life. He leads them to settle down at ease or for the sake of greater worldly advantages to remove from places where they may be a power for good. Others he causes to flee in discouragement from duty because of opposition or persecution. But all such are regarded by heaven with tenderest pity to every child of God whose voice the enemy of souls had succeeded in silencing.

The question is addressed "What dost thou here?" I commissioned you to go into all the world and preach the gospel to prepare a people for the day of God." Why are you here? Who sent you?" The spirit of idolatry is rife in the world today. Although under the influence of Science and Technology and education it has assumed forms more refined and attractive than in the days of the past. Every day adds its sorrowful evidence that faith in the sure word of prophecy is decreasing and in its stead superstition and satanic witchery are captivating the minds of many.

Scene 11

The Great Call to Elisha

God had revealed his plan that Elijah should anoint Elisha son *of Shamhat to succeed him in his place as prophet. Elijah is no more a worn out and tired man, now, he looks very much relieved and a happy prophet, shortly would be getting his assistant, who would finally succeed him. So, Elijah is on his way to find Elisha. As he is journeying northward, he could see amazing scenes realizing how they were a short while ago. That time the ground was parched due to drought and famine. Farming was at a grinding halt in all those areas since neither rain nor dew had fallen for three and half years. Now it was all a changed. It was all green everywhere and the vegetation was springing up completely changing the tragic past reality of drought and famine.*

Finally, Elijah arrived at Abel-meholah where Elisha, son of Shamhat lived. On his arrival itself, Elijah could see a young man energetically plowing with twelve yokes of oxen, himself was driving twelfth pair in the field, with his father's servants. He identified the young man as Elisha. His aged parents, father and mother noticed the elderly man, wearing a garment of hair and a belt approaching their son. They identified the visitor as prophet Elijah from his very clothes, known to the people. They also watched, Elijah cast upon the young man's shoulder the mantle of consecration, a symbolic action of anointment. The elderly couple understood their son was anointed for God's work. So, their son Elisha may leave them. They prepared themselves to accept God's will for Elisha. Elisha was stunned and understood he has been called for God's service, so he must join prophet Elijah. Elisha left the oxen abruptly.

Elisha (Running towards Elijah). Let me kiss my father and mother good-bye and then I will come with you.

Elijah: Go back again for what have I done to thee?

(Elisha leaves him and reaches his parents, who are mentally prepared to part from their beloved son. They find no reason to speak. Elisha arranges a feast for his family members. After the feast Elisha goes to his father embraces and kisses him and same thing with his mother and bids good-bye, only their eyes communicate, without any word, to leave with Elijah. Both Elijah and Elisha walk together praising in heart, for the great call to serve the Lord).

Sub Scene

Short Session of Rabbis

(Hearing the fast events taking place, Rabbis from Bethel, Jericho and Gilgal from the School of prophets and active worshippers of Jehovah from various places of Israel assemble to share the events that took place during the past one year. As per their custom they greet and embrace each other, the symbol of brotherly love. The Senior Rabbi from the School of Jericho is invited to begin their session of sharing).

Senior Rabbi from Jericho: I greet you all in the name of our Lord the Almighty God Jehovah. All glory and honour are for him for ever and ever. I would like to begin with the important event of anointing Elisha by prophet Elijah. It is truly God's consecration. Elisha has been trained by the Lord for this call from birth onwards. Son of a wealthy farmer and a staunch believer who worshipped the true God with his whole family even during the time of persecution and torture of the believers They never bowed down to Baal at the time of universal apostasy and even at the time of threats to their lives. Theirs was a home where the faith of ancient Israel to worship the only true God was the rule of daily life. Elisha was born in such a family whose early life was passed amidst the quietude of country life, under the teaching of God and nature and the discipline of useful work. There Elisha received the training in habits of simplicity and of obedience to his parents and to God that helped to fit him for the high position he had afterwards to occupy. Elisha received the prophetic call while he was with his father's servants joining in their daily work of plowing. Elisha was always, ready to take any work at hand.

Senior Rabbi of Bethel: May I be permitted to add some more facts. He possessed both the capabilities of a leader among men and the humbleness ready to serve. Although he is of a quiet and gentle spirit but energetic and steadfast. He possessed in natural manner the integrity, fidelity and love and fear for God. In such humbleness, in daily routine of jobs, Elisha gained strength of purpose and nobleness of character with them constantly increasing in grace and knowledge. With his obedience to his father in day to day works he was training to obey and do the will of God, with no refusal. With his faithfulness in little things Elisha has prepared for mighty assignments of God. He learned to serve and in learning this he learned also how to instruct and lead. None can know what God's purpose in his discipline may be, but all may be certain that faithfulness in little things is the evidence of fitness for greater responsibilities. Every act of life is a revelation of character. God honors such servants with higher service Elijah had been God's instrument for the overthrow of gigantic evils Therefore, in due course Elisha had been anointed to become a co-worker with Elijah to be trained for greater works. The idolatry supported by Ahab and the heathen Jezebel had seduced the nation, but that evil was checked by Elijah on Mount Carmel. Baal was given a death blow. The people of Israel had been deeply stirred and were returning to worship the true God, the only one God. Now it had fallen on the shoulders of Elisha, the successor to Elijah to carefully and patiently guide Israel in safe path not to turn again to idol worship by instigation of Satan. This is the only important news for us to share for the time being.

Scene 12

Covetousness and Murder

King Ahab is surveying the vineyard of Naboth - a Jezeerlite, from his summer palace. This is like that of King David who watched Bathsheba bathing from his palace. King David broke several commandments of God coveting another man's wife and committing adultery, followed his deception, telling lies and finally murdering Uriah the Hittite, the most faithful soldier - the husband of Bathsheba, in a most possible wicked way. Here, the scene is with covetousness for property of another man - an ordinary citizen Naboth, who can be ordered by the King to obey, or even harassed and killed. The vineyard of Naboth is wearing the beauty of heaven since it received the rain after three and half years drought. Ahab sends his messenger to call Naboth. Naboth presents before the King, as a humble citizen with due respect for the King.

Ahab: (With a decisive tone, not noticing the reaction of Naboth). Let me have your vineyard to use for a vegetable garden since it is close to my palace in exchange I will give you a better vineyard or if you prefer will pay whatever it is worth.

Naboth: (In a confused and tense filled tone). The Lord forbid that I should give you the inheritance of my fathers.

(King Ahab, without any more talk with Naboth, enters his house heavy and displeased in heart, because of the word which Naboth had spoken to him. He lays down on his bed and turns away his face; and refuses to eat his bread. Jezebel gets all the information about the deal on Naboth's vineyard and becomes wild, then enters the room of her husband. Jezebel is a master in deceptions to accumulate wealth by grabbing and by sending criminals to frighten or to kill the property owners, she has a kingdom of her own with such greedily acquired illegal properties, maniac mad woman).

Jezebel: Why are you so sullen? Why don't you eat?

Ahab: (In hopeless mood and voice). Because I said to Naboth the Jezerite sell me your vineyard or if prefer will give you another vineyard in its place. But he said I will not give you my vineyard. (Leaves long breath - out of frustration).

Jezebel: (Nagging Ahab) Is this how you act as king over Israel? Get up and eat, cheer up. We will get you the vineyard of Naboth the Jezerite.

(After consoling and assuring her husband, Jezebel gets into a most dubious and heinous crime of making letters in the name of Ahab and placing his seal on them and sends that letter to the elders and nobles who lived in Naboth's city with him. That fake letter orders the Elders and Nobles to take part in the worst crime in the eyes of God).

One of the Nobles reads out the letter: Dear Elders and Nobles I am reading out the letter of our King Ahab, proclaim a day of fasting and seat Naboth in a prominent place among the people. But seat two scoundrels opposite him and have them testify that he has cursed both God and the king. Then take him out and stone him to death.

(On hearing the letter, they are shocked to imagine enacting the scene ruthlessly and unethically. None of them open their mouths, an indication that they have been pushed to commit the crime of stoning an innocent man-Naboth).

The Same Noble: Let us do so as instructed by our King Ahab. (So, the elders and the nobles who lived in Naboth's city did as Jezebel directed them, as per the letter. They proclaimed a fast and seated Naboth in a prominent place among the people. Then two scoundrels came and sat opposite him, and enacted the dubious plan of Jezebel).

Scoundrel Number One: May the curse of the Lord befall on us. What made you invite Naboth for this fast and give a prominent seat among us? He does not deserve to be in our congregation because I had witnessed that he had blasphemed the Holy name of the Lord in a degrading language. He said that there are many more gods more powerful than Jehovah and then he cursed God and the king. My friend who is sitting beside me is also a witness for this blasphemy.

Scoundrel Number Two: Yes, I am a witness for the blasphemy of God of Israel not only that he also blasphemed and dishonored our King as a weak and foolish king and also questioned his authority. He commented on his personal life he must be stoned to death as per our Law and Custom.

(Naboth becomes speechless and nervous and the death of fear gripped him).

Naboth: No, I have never blasphemed the God of Israel or the King of Israel. I am a law-abiding citizen and love the Lord with my whole heart and soul, body and mind. My country men, you all know that I am a very simple and God-fearing man, never violated the Law of God and committed any sin to dishonor our Lord. Please come for my defence. I do not know these two people who falsely accused me and have not seen them in my life. I am a family man with wife and children please do not put me for the shameful death by stoning. (He cries loudly begging his fellow countrymen, to save him. But no one responds).

The Senior Elder: (In a stern and merciless voice). We must put him on trial. Drag him to the public place meant to stone the blasphemers. Let us tie him to a pole, let us stone him as per the Law who blasphemes our King.

(Despite the louder cry of Naboth with death, realizing the cruel and most painful death by stoning, some strong men drag Naboth to the place of stoning, outside the city. All the people rush following the victim to be stoned to pick up stones from the stones kept ready for stoning).

Naboth: (Cries for help from heaven). O Lord, please save me I am innocent. You know it, please come Lord and save me. I am falsely charged with blasphemy Lord, please, please.

(The people pick up those special lethal stones meant for stoning and hit Naboth. Naboth is being hit by the stones from that crowd. His whole body is targeted, especially his head to kill him, instantly. Naboth is groaning with terrible pain and soon with the fast-bowled stones he falls unconscious and falls to the ground, blood from all over body drips to the ground and runs like a stream. Naboth makes no more cries and dies. The elders find him dead and they immediately inform Jezebel through a messenger). (Their messenger reaches Jezebel with the news of Naboth's death).

Messenger: (Bowing his head before Jezebel). Naboth has been stoned and is dead. (This news makes Jezebel extremely happy and she runs to her husband to revive him to normalcy and to bring him to happy mood).

Jezebel: Get up, take possession of the vineyard of Naboth the Jezerite that he refused to sell you. He is no longer alive but dead.

(The moment he heard the news about Naboth's death, he jumped from his bed with happiness. He did not inquired about the cause of death).

Ahab: Is it so? What good news for me! Now, I will go and grab that vineyard (Ahab rushes to grab Naboth's vineyard).

Scene 13

God Deputes his Lion Elijah

The king is not allowed to enjoy un-rebuked that which he had gained by fraudulent method and the bloodshed of Naboth. The word of the Lord comes to Elijah.

The Voice of God to Elijah: Arise go down to meet Ahab king of Israel who is in Samaria. Behold he is in the vineyard of Naboth. Whither he has gone down to possess it. And thou shall speak unto him, saying, "Thus, saith the Lord: Have you not murdered a man and seized his property?' This is what the Lord says, in the place where the dogs licked up Naboth's blood, dogs will lick up your blood, yes yours."

(Elijah bows down on receiving the message from the Lord and reaches King Ahab to deliver the message immediately).

Elijah: (Stands in front of King Ahab and says). Thus saith the Lord: Have you not murdered a man and seized his property? This is what the Lord says in the place where dogs licked up Naboth's blood, dogs will lick up your blood yes yours

Ahab: (Angrily). So you have found my enemy?

Elijah: I have found you because you have sold yourself to do evil in the eyes of the Lord. The Lord's message is 'I am going to bring disaster on you. I will consume your descendants and cut off from Ahab every male in Israel slave or free. I will make your house like that of Jeroboam, son of Nebat and that of Baasha son of Ahijah because you have provoked me to anger and have caused Israel to sin and also concerning Jezebel the Lord says " Dogs will devour Jezebel by the wall of Jezreel dogs will eat those belongings of Ahab who die in the city and the birds of the air will feed on those who die in the country.

(On hearing these fearful words of the Lord through prophet Elijah, Ahab tears down his clothes and puts on sackcloth and fasts, to escape from such curse and punishment from the Lord. He goes around meekly, around as a symbol of his repentance and fasting to obtain the mercy of God. The merciful and forgiving God sends his message to prophet Elijah).

Voice of God: Have you noticed how Ahab has humbled himself before me? Because he has humbled himself will not bring this disaster in his day, but I will bring it on his house in the days of his son.

(Prophet Elijah becomes speechless, in wonder and surprises at God's most merciful dealings with forgiveness).

Scene 14

Echo of Naboth's Murder and Greedy and Monstrous Jezebel

The School of Prophets at Jericho

The Senior Rabbis of Schools of prophets at Bethel and Gilgal arrive with their students to attend the meet scheduled at Jericho, after the death of Naboth, to exchange the latest happenings in Israel and its impacts on the Israelites.

Senior Rabbi of Jericho's School of Prophets: Beloved Senior Rabbis of Bethel and Gilgal and dear students. I greet you and welcome you all in the Holy Name of our Lord. We are meeting after one year or so. This meet has a special condolence reference to Naboth, a God fearing and peace loving man who was known for his hospitality and availability for his neighbors in any trouble. Such a noble soul was stoned to death and met with the most painful and shameful death for no fault of any sort. The crime was committed due to the greed or covetousness breaking of the Ten Commandments. Ahab did evil in the eyes of the Lord than any of those before him. Ahab knew very well the seizure or compulsory purchase of land was illegal in Israel. A man's heritage had to be handed on to the next generation.

But other people's right do not bother Jezebel she quietly arranged for Naboth's death by stoning him. By manipulating blasphemous charges on the innocent Naboth. She has only to contrive a blasphemy charge backed by the statutory number of witnesses to forfeit the criminal's land. The whole of Israel has come to know the diabolical murderous act of Jezebel the wife of Ahab who had no remorse of conscience in seizing the coveted vine yard of Naboth in the most unjust manner. With this introduction, I request the Senior Rabbi from the School of Prophets of Bethel to explain the impacts on the morale of Israelites and the dishonor caused to the Lord by breaking his Commandments.

(Thus, he invites the Senior Rabbi of Bethel, who continues the subject).

Senior Rabbi of Bethel: Thank you for this introduction. Ahab has proved himself as the worst and cruel king in the history of Israel due to his own lack of devotion to our Lord and his marriage with Jezebel the great idol worshipper, whose father pioneered in propagating the idol worship of Baal. Therefore, every commandment of our Lord is likely to be broken and violated by the future generation or the citizens of Israel. "Like the people their leader" is proverbial but henceforth it will be "like the king the people in Israel.

Ahab during his life time was trying to change the ideal covenant structure of Yahweh's society into a system prevalent in the neighboring pagan nations. His wife Jezebel's only goal in life is to destroy the faith in Yahweh and the Yahweh worship replacing it with the Baal worship along with it. The idols of Ashtoreth all due to the inspiration of the evil spirit or Satan the devil. As a result, trying to destroy the sacred plan of Yahweh to nurture Israel as a holy nation and light to all the nations on the earth.

Ahab has set a dangerous precedence by killing and confiscating the property of Naboth who a true Israelite with reverence for family inheritance was. How can a king with such diabolical influence of his wife stoop so low to murder a law abiding and God-fearing citizen just to covet his property?

Then twisting the Israel Law on blasphemy to achieve personal goal without any remorse of conscience nor any fear of the God of Israel? Godless Ahab broke the Commandments by coveting the neighbor's property by scheming false witnesses to murder the property owner Naboth. That murderous plan was authored by his idol worshipping godless wife Jezebel, who had no such commandments to regulate the moral life in idol worship. A king has innumerable properties at his disposal. So where was the need for him to covet the property of his own citizen to fulfill his evil desire?

Naboth was falsely accused of blasphemy with two false witnesses and was stoned to death. People in power think that they can do anything and everything using their influence and money and they do not mind killing ordinary people like Naboth to meet their ends. But the Almighty God, the most righteous judge cannot accept if any injustice was done for the powerless and helpless people. His eyes are watching all such wicked actions of the people and he has his own ways and time to take revenge on behalf of the victims and duly punish wicked ones. In case of Naboth, the Lord was quick in sending his servant Elijah to condemn the murder of an innocent man to grab his property. The same Lord is watchful on every human being more importantly on the wellbeing of the poor and helpless people. He takes up their cause to punish the oppressors and wicked people not in the pattern of Naboth's case. The Lord punishes the greedy and merciless murderers in his own ways. In this regard, no one can escape from the eyes of the Lord.

Rabbi of Gilgal: May I please be permitted to say few words? Ahab and his wife Jezebel used the Law of ancient East that the property of rebels and public criminals falls into the hands of the king. His greed for property will sow seeds for rulers, officials, business people. So, all will pervert the justice to grab the properties of innocent citizens. God's plan for every person to have his/her own land or property will be diluted and nullified by using the Law and the future will produce landless and homeless citizens all over the world and there will be Tower of Babel type tall buildings across the world to hide the sun and the moon for the future generations. History repeats itself is proverbial in the same history of Israel in the past King David by chance set his eye from his palace on the woman who was bathing in her home. Lust made him blind and godless which made him break three Commandments of God, coveting another man's wife, committing debauchery with her and finally murdering her husband with utmost wickedness to possess the woman for himself. After all, as a king he had beautiful women in his royal harem, but he grabbed the wife of another man one of the most faithful soldier in his army. Thus, he made his citizens, the Israelites forget or ignore the Commandments of the Lord to fulfill their sexual desires by hook or crook. King David opened the chapter of sexual immorality and murder to achieve it in Israel. Such heinous sex crimes may grow in humans and ripen in future with rapes to gang rapes not even sparing children and elderly women in the world. Murder of Naboth is only the beginning to human history such murders of innocent people to grab their properties will continue till eternity. Also, there will be the clan of Jezebel to play politics to suppress the truth and to encourage evil in every sphere of life ultimately to promote devil worship with lot many worldly pleasures to misguide humanity. The sign of devil worship or idol worship is progression of sexual immorality and greed for money or for the property of all those who sold their souls to enjoy the pleasures of this world and would become idol worshippers supported by witchcraft and human sacrifice and all such inhuman activities inspired by the evil spirit with Satan as the master.

Their hearts and souls will become insensitive to the Commandments of the Lord to lead a holy life and to attract the people of other nations to prepare them to walk to Zion where the Law of the Lord will be given to them to guide their lives. Ahab is a striking example of the incredible obduracy of the human heart. Ahab married the despicable Jezebel, Phoenician princess who propagated the religion and culture of the Canaanite gods in Israel chiefly of Baal and Ashtoreth. With this Jezebel attracted the weak in faith to become worshippers of fertility gods, masters of sex, rain and harvest coupled with cultic prostitution. Many Israelites were lured into this pagan culture and worship.

Rabbi of Jericho: May I please be allowed to add few information. The word 'prostitution' means for the people of Jehovah physical sex as well as infidelity to Yahweh. Ahab set up an altar for Baal in the temple of Baal which he built in Samaria and made an Asherah pole. Ahab did everything that could make the Lord angry, even more than any of the kings of Israel, who ruled before him. The same Ahab and his wife Jezebel have become a cult due to the inducement of carnal joys and free sex and freedom to loot and grab illegal properties to that population that were deviated or thrown away. Commandments of our

Lord and the worship of our Lord the true God.

A Senior Student from Jericho: May I please be permitted to say something which are in secret float among the ordinary masses?

Chief Rabbi of Jericho: (with a smile). Yes, you are permitted to say what you heard from the masses.

Senior Student : I heard from the people whenever the Royal couple pass the citizens get emotionally charged and shout, "Hail our Queen" ignoring the King, the vivacious queen responds with a tempting smile sometimes winking at " Hail our Queen". Jezebel enjoys such adoration knowing fully well it is her vivacious beauty that inspires the citizens. Further, I heard they greet her from their lips but in secret they commit mental debauchery with their queen keeping their beautiful queen in their imaginations and kissing her passionately with wild emotions all in secret.

(The whole congregation was aghast looking at each other silently in a shell-shocked condition).

Chief Rabbi of Jericho: I am ashamed to hear such filthy and vulgar information from your mouth that too a student from my School. I seriously condemn your action. As a student of our School you have better things to notice and to learn but not such demoralizing information.

Schools of Prophets were established to prepare and train future servants of God whose behavior should be most refined and acceptable to the people of God. I am ashamed that your ears have received such vulgar information and your brain preserved it to leak it out in a very wrong place (The student kneels repenting his action. The Congregation feel sorry for his disturbed spirit. The Chief Rabbi plans to bring normalcy to the atmosphere. So, with a smile). Any how you are pardoned but do not do such thing, like those demoralized citizens. (The whole congregations breaks into laughter).

Chief Rabbi of Bethel: Excuse me for my intervention with due humbility. I request the Chief Rabbi of Jericho to take back his censuring words on the student. In my opinion, we must allow them to speak whatever they hear whether good or bad. Moreover, Satan's diabolical mischief is to destroy the law and order everywhere and to convert all human beings enslaved to meaner sexual sins like beasts.

Nothing shocking in his statement about Queen Jezebel who did not maintain her royal dignity as a queen but all the while exposing herself as vivacious and tempting women not minding the society of men whether royal or commoners on the streets. She wants to win the people not with her moral beauty but with her soul corrupting physical beauty.

The Student: Honorable Rabbis with free mind, I accept very humbly the censure of Chief Rabbi and beg pardon from all of you for my foolishness. I am sorry (The Chief Rabbi of Jericho takes the student by hand and hugs him, with a sign of pardon).

Chief Rabbi of Jericho: So, it is confirmed. That the people are worshipping the King and his wife along with Baal who have granted them full freedom to lead sinful lives breaking all the Commandments of God. After the death of Ahab sure Jezebel will dominate the nation directly or diabolically. She will repeat the scheme of killing Naboth to kill all the rich people or property owners to amass unimaginable quantum of landed properties and gold and silver like a mad woman thoroughly enjoying in amassing properties.

Chief Rabbi of Bethel: May I add few more facts? The people say that she uses the King's name to take heavy bribes to sanction any of Kingdom's big works. She has amassed gold and silver through bribes more than what lies there in the royal treasury. But she has buried them in different places including in forests and no one knows the earmarks except Jezebel. She never discloses anything about her illegal properties to anyone since she is afraid of her own life that there are people to murder her to grab all her illegally earned properties including gold and silver buried. She is also allowing her followers to do the same thing to loot the followers of Jehovah, the true God of Israel. We can expect all such developments in the future, Israel destroying its culture and spiritual heredity and finally making the true Israelites landless and homeless, second-class citizens in their own nation.

Under the Satanic rule there will be evil in the court rooms throughout the world courts of law will be corrupt. Only Jehovah will judge everyone both good and bad for all their deeds. The followers of Baal and Jezebel harass, suppress the true Israelites to the extent of killing them on various pretexts using all the government machineries for this massacre or genocide.

Chief Rabbi of Gilgal: Unfortunately, the "Hail Queen" culture to greet Jezebel will pass from one generation to another generation with ulterior meaning, "Let the Queen also loot, and her followers or admirers also loot". To keep alive the immoral way of life with their idol worship which will encourage them to practice Satanic witchcraft and human sacrifice to please satan to get whatever they want more importantly wealth and with wealth buying the beautiful women to gratify their unquenchable lusts.

There will be towers of Babel's all over the earth by building tall buildings which will disallow the free flow of fresh air to the people. A time will come the children may not be able to know the sun and the moon due to the tall buildings above their heads everywhere. When the true God rules our lives, we can see peace and joy in having brotherly love with one another and not having any wickedness to ill-treat or to rule over neighbors. All will live in peace praising God in their daily lives and obeying his commands. Such an atmosphere will endorse the rule of God on the earth. We have been called by God to work for that and proclaim it so the wicked one, the Satan may not lure the people to lead immoral lives and to make demi-gods among mortal men and women. The entire humanity can be saved only through divine intervention, yes only the Lord bring changes.

Chief Rabbi of Gilgal: It is very true; let us all pray to the Lord continuously for his Divine intervention to save the universe and humanity created by him.

Scene 15

King Ahaziah Succeeds King Ahab

King Ahaziah succeeds King Ahab. He did evil in the eyes of the Lord, because he walked in the ways of his father and mother and caused Israel to sin. He served and worshipped Baal and provoked the Lord, the God of Israel, to anger, just as his father had done. After Ahab's death Moab rebelled against Israel. During this period of turmoil Ahaziah had fallen through the lattice of his upper room in Samaria and severely injured, struck with death fear and confined to his bed. Therefore, he called his messengers.

Ahaziah (Orders his messengers). Go and consult Baal-zebub, the God of Ekron, to see if I will recover from this injury.

(The messengers bow down to the King and depart to meet Baal-Zebub). During this moment the angel of the Lord said to Elijah with a message.

Angel: Go up and meet the messengers of the King of Samaria and ask them, 'Is it because there is no God in Israel that you are going off to consult Baal-zebub, the god of Ekron? Therefore, this is what the Lord says: 'You will not leave the bed you are lying on. "You will certainly die."

(So, Elijah met the messengers and passed the message. The messengers received the frightening message and returned to the King).

King Ahaziah: (Inquires from the messengers). Why have you come back?

One of the Messengers: A man came to meet us and he said to us, 'Go back to the King who sent and tell him "This is what the Lord says :Is it because there is no God in Israel that you are sending men to consult Baal-zebub, the god of Ekron? Therefore, you will not leave the bed you are lying on. You will certainly die."

(On hearing the message King Ahaziah gets upset with death fear and profusely sweats and become anxious).

King Ahazia: What kind of man was he who came to meet you and told you this?

One of the messengers: He was a man with garment of hair and a leather belt around his waist.

King Ahaziah: That was Elijah the Tishbite.

King Ahaziah: (Orders his Captain). Captain go with a company of fifty men to Elijah.

(Captain bows down to the King and hurries with his contingent of fifty men to meet Elijah. He finds Elijah sitting at the top of a hill and climbs to meet him).

Captain: (On reaching Elijah). Man of God the King says, 'Come down.

Elijah: (Replies the Captain). If I am a man of God, may fire come down from heaven and consume you and your fifty men. (The fire falls from heaven, consumes the Captain and his fifty men).

(King Ahaziah receives this shocking news but dares to send one more team of fifty men under a Captain to Elijah. The Captain with his fifty men rush to meet Elijah on the top of the hill).

Captain: (In a stern voice). Man of God, this is what the King says, 'Come down at once'.

Elijah: If I am a man of God. May fire come down from heaven and consume you and your fifty men.

(Fire from God falls on the Captain and his fifty men and consume them).

(King Ahaziah is still adamant to get Elijah, so, he sends another team of fifty men under a Captain. But the third Captain on reaching the hill top falls on his knees before Elijah and pleads).

Third Captain: Man of God please have respect for my life and the lives of these fifty men your servants! See, fire has fallen from heaven and consumed the first two captains and all their men. But now have respect for my life.

(At this juncture, Elijah hears the voice of the angel of God).

Angel: Go down with him; do not be afraid of him.

(Elijah comes down from the hill and goes with the Captain to meet the King to deliver the message, himself. On reaching the King, who was lying in bed, Elijah delivers the message).

Elijah: This is what the Lord says, "Is it is because there is no God in Israel for you to consult that you have sent messengers to consult Baal-zebub, the god of Ekron? Because you have done this, you will never leave the bed you are lying on. You will certainly die."

(King Ahaziah died so in his bed as per the word of God, communicated through Prophet Elijah).

Scene 16

Urgent Session of Rabbis on King Ahaziah

(After formal greetings, Chief Rabbi of Gilgal opens the sharing session)

Chief Rabbi of Gilgal: Thank you for giving me this opportunity to narrate some more serious incidents in Israel and the role of prophet Elijah in them. King Ahaziah succeeded his father King Ahab. And some news spread that Prophet Elijah had called fire from heaven and burnt down two contingents of men of Ahaziah. Elijah has become famous for calling fire from heaven to burn.

One Senior Student: (Making a joke). Therefore the people say that nobody dares to go before Elijah afraid of death by fire from heaven.

Rabbi of Gilgal: (Smiling). No, no Elijah is a harmless soul he can never harm anyone with fire or sword. He knows only one thing that is to carry out the command of God Almighty. In fact, Elijah is our role model to stand for God and to honour his name in all situations not minding personal safety at the same time relying on God with unshakable faith in all odds and dangerous situations. Prophet Elijah is an embodiment of faith and love for God who can never allow the Lord's name to be dishonored by anyone in any circumstances. There can be no rival to the God of Israel and if the people including the king violate this fundamental principle of faith, Elijah is the weapon in the hands of God to teach them lesson sometimes very harsh lesson as instruments of God. I would like to narrate a recent incident in Israel. Ahab was saved from the judgment of God since he repented. After his death, his son Ahaziah became the king of Israel. After his coronation the old enemy of Israel, Moab rebelled against Israel. In that moment, of crisis, in Samaria King Ahaziah fell through the window from the upper room of his palace and was badly injured. He sent messengers to consult Baal-zebub the god of Ekron to know whether he would survive or face death. Foolishness is also a sin which is normally ignored. Ahaziah cannot be ignorant to what happened on Mount Carmel during the time of his father's regime. Elijah had demonstrated to the entire Israel that the God of Israel as the only one true God and the idols like Baal have no power, but instruments created by Satan the devil to deviate the Israelites from their true faith. Elijah put up the grand show of halting the rain and dew for more than three and half years as punishment from God for the Israelites for their idol worship of Baal. And again, he challenged the bringing of fire from heaven and proved the Baal worshippers as on the wrong track misguided by their king Ahab and his wife Jezebel. Again, he prayed from the top of Mount Carmel to send rain. God obliged Elijah and sent rain. These incidents have become history in the records of Israel and the Baal worshippers started coming back to Jehovah with their repentance. Even King Ahab father of Ahaziah repented with sack cloth and fasting therefore he was spared from the serious curse of Jehovah to have a painful and shameful death. The question is how was King Ahaziah ignorant about these great events on Mount Carmel and the power of Elijah the great prophet of God? God's demonstration of his power on Mount Carmel had become a daily talk in every Israelite's home. Ahaziah provoked the God of Israel in a very foolish and casual way by sending messengers to consult Baal-zebub the god of Ekron to know whether he would survive. Instead had he submitted himself to the God of Israel pleading for mercy to save his life he would have been saved. May I please request the Chief Rabbi of Bethel to continue further narrations.

Rabbi of Bethel: As you please why not? King Ahaziah has done another foolish act he did not send his messengers with a humble request to call prophet Elijah instead he sent a small contingent of soldiers under a captain as though to arrest a criminal or to show his pomp and glory. It seems Jehovah felt that the honour of his servant Elijah was hurt by the act of Ahaziah. Therefore, Elijah answered the captain as per the words put in his mouth by God. "If I am a man of God, may fire come down from heaven and devour you and your men. Immediately fire came down from heaven and devoured the captain and his men. The news of the fate of his men under a Captain might have reached the king. Ahaziah knew how God demonstrated his power with fire on Mount Carmel answering the prayer of Elijah. Even now he had not realized that he was playing with the God of Israel, whose authority can neither be ignored nor undermined. But he once again sent fifty men under a captain to Elijah with the same message. That team of men also met the same fate of devoured by the fire from heaven. Ahaziah sent one more contingent of fifty men under a Captain to Elijah. But that captain was a wise and humble man, therefore he fell on his knees and begged Elijah to spare his life and also the lives of fifty men. So, they were not devoured were by fire from heaven. Then the angel of the Lord said to

Elijah, "Go down with him and do not be afraid". So he stood up and went down with him to the king. And Elijah said to the king, "Listen to this word of the Lord. Because you sent your messengers to consult Baal-zebub, the god of Ekron. You shall not rise again from the bed on which you lie but shall surely die." Ahaziah died according to what the Lord had said through the mouth of Elijah. The God of Israel is most merciful. Therefore, he spared the life of Ahab from horrible death since he had confessed. But the Lord is against the proud and rebels. What Ahaziah did was a sort of rebellion by not honoring the God of Israel and his most faithful servant prophet Elijah. Ahaziah was returning to idol worship by seeking favor from Baalzebub, the god of Ekron. Rather, he was trying to nullify the will of God demonstrated through his most faithful servant Elijah to save the Israelites from idol Worship which would finally take them to break all the Divine commands. Laws and decrees of God and to lead beastly, immoral lives of dishonoring the Creator and having no respect for the lives of fellow human beings, instead following the degraded carnal life to please Satan in the way of the neighboring heathen nations. Therefore, the most righteous Lord punished King Ahaziah. There can be no change in the nature or character of the God of Israel. He knew idol worship will ruin the souls of Israelites they will sell their souls for wealth, sex and positions and would become a bad example to the heathen nations to lead such immoral and godless life.

Rabbi of Jericho: We are thankful to the Chief Rabbi of Bethel for enlightening us on the reason for Prophet Elijah to get fire from heaven to devour the two contingents led by Captains of King Ahaziah. It was once again God's action to save the people from idol worship which would lead to break down the Divine Commands, laws and decrees finally resulting in immoral and unspiritual people. This clears and reasons why there was once again fire power demonstrated by Elijah as per God's plan. All glory and honour be for the God of Israel for ever and ever. I would like to invite Chief Rabbi of Gilgal to narrate the ministry of Elijah and Elisha and some rumours spreading fast about the final days of prophet Elijah.

Chief Rabbi of Gilgal: I am thankful for this invitation but bit confusing! For several years after the call of Elisha. Elijah and Elisha labored together, the younger man daily gaining greater preparedness for his work. As Elijah's successor, Elisha by careful patient instruction ought to prepare to guide Israel in safe paths. His association with Elijah the greatest prophet since the day of Moses prepared him for the work that he was soon to take up alone. Ever since he joined prophet Elijah his training has started in practical terms he was with his master in every occasion and trained to be fearless and to seek only the will of God and his honour not minding the perils in such service. Also, Elijah took Elisha to our Schools of Prophets established by Samuel at Gilgal. Bethel and Jericho which have fallen into decay during the years of Israel's apostasy. Elijah re-established these Schools wherein we are associated to make provisions for young men to gain education that would lead them to magnify the Law and make it honorable. Especially, he did instruct them concerning their high privilege of loyally maintaining their allegiance to the God of heaven. He also impressed on their minds the importance of letting simplicity mark every feature of their education. Only in this way, could they receive the mold of heaven and go forth to work in the ways of the Lord. I feel Chief Rabbi of Jericho is in a better position to narrate the later developments and speculations.

Chief Rabbi of Jericho: To start with be ready to hear about a sad point. I shall come to it later. It is very fruitful for this very remarkable meet since we discuss and keep informed each other whatever has been happened in Israel and among the chosen people and God's intervention through prophet Elijah to correct them and to bring them back to fit them into his holy will for the people of Israel to become a shining example, so the people of heathen nations receive the knowledge of his Commandments to lead a just and righteous life which should spread to the entire world. Now coming to the sad point to mention some of us received the revelation that prophet Elijah is going to be taken up to heaven very soon this revelation has been given many of us may be in other Schools of prophets too a spiritual frenzy. It is more likely the end of his mission may come in a mysterious way since death cannot overcome a man who burned with zealous love for the Lord. Elijah is representing those who at the close of earth's history will be changed from mortal to immortal and be transported to heaven without seeing death. During his mission in the desert in loneliness and discouragement he prayed that he might die. But Lord in his mercy had not taken him at his word. There was yet a great work for Elijah to do and when his work was done, he was not to perish in discouragement and solitude. Not for him the descent into tomb but the ascent with God's angels to the presence of his glory. During these years of united ministry. Elijah from time to time was called upon to meet flagrant evils with stern rebuke. When wicked Ahab seized Naboth's vineyard it was the voice of Elijah that prophesied his doom and his house hold. And when Ahaziah after the death of his father Ahab turned from the living God to Baalzebub, the god of Ekron it was Elijah's voice that was heard once more in earnest protest. Those who undertake this training of young workers are doing noble service. And the young men to whom the word of consecration has been spoken whose privilege it is to be brought into close association with earnest, godly workers should make the most of their opportunity. God has honored them by choosing them for his service and by placing them where they can gain greatest fitness for it and they should be humble, faithful, obedient and willing to sacrifice. If they submit to God's discipline carrying out his directions and choosing his servants as counselors they will develop into righteous, high principled steadfast men whom God can entrust with responsibilities.

Chief Rabbi of Gilgal: Of course, it is true even some of the students at Jericho had such revelation on Elijah regarding his mysterious departure from the world.Even Elisha during his visit to our School with Elijah had spoken with me with his heavy heart that he too received such revelation regarding Elijah that he would be taken away in some mysterious way. Therefore, Elisha is not leaving his master rather sticking on closely to him with grief in heart to face such sudden separation.

Scene 17

God Glorifies Elijah
His Faithful Servant

Elijah is on his round of service accompanied by Elisha from School to School. Now they are on their way from Gilgal. Elisha is walking with Elijah with heavy heart, sure of the event to take place that Elijah would be taken away, suddenly, in some mysterious way. Elijah too aware of the event waiting for his separation from Elisha and the time to leave this world. It would be God's will; therefore, he is maintaining the serenity in his face.

Elijah: (Looking at Elisha). Stay here the Lord has sent me to Bethel.

Elisha: (Understanding it as an indication to test him whether he would be tempted to give up his resolution and to go back to his home, to join his family or discouraged). As surely as the Lord lives and as you live, I will not leave you.

(Now the tired servant of the man of God is keeping close to Elisha. They reach the School at Bethel. Some of the prophets at Bethel meet Elisha, when he was not with the prophet Elijah).

Prophets of Bethel: (Hurriedly speak). Do you know that the Lord is going to take your master from you today?

One prophet out of them: The revelation has been given to us and also to you that Elijah would be taken away today but this revelation has not been given to Elijah so far it looks!

Elisha: (With the agony reflecting in his face). Yes I know but do not speak of it.

Elijah: (After spending little time in Bethel, tells Elisha). Stay here, Elisha the Lord has sent me to Jericho.

Elisha (Controlling his emotions within). Surely as the Lord lives and as you live. I will not leave you.

 (So, they reach Jericho. The moment they reached Jericho some of the prophets of Jericho meet Elisha).

Prophets of Jericho: Do you know that the Lord is going to take your master from you today?

Elisha: (In sad voice). Yes, I know but do not speak of it.

Elijah: (After some time, Elijah again tells him). Stay here the Lord has sent me to the Jordan.

Elisha: (In discouraged agonizing tone). As surely as the Lord lives and as you live, I will not leave you.

 (So, the two of them walk on. Fifty men of the company of the prophets walk and stand at a distance, facing the place where Elijah and Elisha had stopped at Jordan. Elijah takes his mantle, rolls it up and strikes the water with it. The water divides to the right and left, and the two of them cross over on dry ground).

Elijah says to Elisha: (After crossed Jordon). "Tell me what I can do for you before I am taken from you?" (Knowing fully well Elisha is not going to ask for any worldly honour or for a high place among the great men of earth).

Elisha: I pray thee, let a double portion of thy spirit be upon me.
Elijah: (With love and inexpressible emotions). You have asked a difficult thing yet if you see me when I am taken from you it will be yours otherwise not.

(As they were walking along and talking together, suddenly a chariot of fire and horses of fire appear and separate the two and Elijah taken up to heaven in a whirlwind).

Elisha: (Seeing this helplessly, cries out loudly, in heartbroken condition). My father my father! The chariots of Israel and its charioteers).

(Elisha looks up and searches for Elijah, but can see him no more. Then he takes his own clothes and tears them as a symbol of unbearable agony. He picks up the mantle that fell from Elijah, when he was taken up. He walks towards the banks of the Jordan river.

Elisha: Where now is the Lord the God of Elijah? (Then he strikes the water, it divides to right and to the left, and he crosses it).

The company of the prophets from Jericho, who were watching say to one another: The spirit of Elijah is resting on Elisha.

They come and on meeting Elisha they bow down to the ground and say: Look we your servants have fifty able men. Let them go and look for your master. Perhaps the Spirit of the Lord has picked him up and set him down on some mountain or in some valley.

Elisha: (In very confident voice). No do not send them.

(But they persist Elisha, for that search mission and pleads to oblige them).

Elisha: (In a disinterested voice). Send them.

(Those fifty men look for Elijah for three days but do not find him. They return to Elisha with their sad faces or with disappointed spirit).

One of the search team: (Bowing down). We searched for prophet Elijah in forests and on the tops of the mountains during the last three days, but we didn't find him, so we have returned discouraged and sorrowful to inform you.

Elisha: (After listening, looking at the Heaven and leaving a long breath with tears rolling down). Didn't I tell you not to go.

(Elisha keeping the mantle of Elijah on his shoulder, walks alone, to continue the ministry of Elijah; entrusted upon him by the Lord).

www.ingramcontent.com/pod-product-compliance
Lightning Source LLC
Chambersburg PA
CBHW031136160726
47987CB00026B/828